Dead is Best

By

Jo Perry

Fahrenheit Press

For A & I

With thanks to Tama Winograd for her help with this book and her work on behalf of animals, and gratitude to Chris McVeigh for taking a chance on Charles and Rose.

". . . death is the seed from which I grow."

William Burroughs

Chapter 1

"Most of the people I admire . . . are either dead or not feeling well."

Tom Waits

The girl wasn't with us and then she was. I could say that she appeared suddenly or like a bat out of hell—but neither evokes the gloomy precipitousness of her arrival.

I was combing the reddish fur on Rose's back with my fingers—then scratching the places behind her ears that she likes scratched—and trying to fully occupy the seamless, boundless Sabbath that is death—at least mine and Rose's.

Then here she is in the middle of our perpetual nowhere looking awful.

She's dressed in black leather leggings and a silvery sleeveless top. Her brown hair has been bleached corn silk yellow and straightened into perfect verticality. But she's blue around the edges—as if she'd dipped her fingers and toes in grape juice—bluish toes and toenails of her pale bare feet, blue lips, and blue-edged nostrils. Her pupils are tiny black pinholes in the glacier-blue of her irises and her thick black eyeliner and mascara just make them seem blacker.

You'd think in death Rose and I would have some fucking privacy. You'd think that having given up the ghost I'd be beyond the grasp of my ex-stepdaughter, the parasite.

Chapter 2

"The dead are way more organized than the living."

China Miéville

Her name is Cali. Cali Green. She was fifteen the last time I saw her—which was at my funeral—during which she was busy texting or applying makeup. That was almost two years ago, more or less—time doesn't exist here. When I was briefly and unfortunately married to her mother, her name was—get this—Cali Green Stone. I'm Stone. Charles Stone. But people always pronounced the last two names as one—Greenstone.

A stupid hippie name like Cali Green Stone might have been a problem for her, but at her fancy schmancy progressive, exclusive, private college preparatory school off Mulholland Drive, that's the kind of name kids had. The parents—oral surgeons and architects and screenwriters and actors and movie directors and rock musicians—were Sallys and Ruths, Steves and Michaels. Yet behold their offspring––Truth, Canyon, Druid, Turquoise, Vanilla and Road. Don't tell me those are names—they're brands.

Those pretentious, fucked-up names are why I decided to name Rose "Rose." "Rose" is beautiful, evocative, delicate, and feminine in a sweet old-fashioned way. And Rose is all these things fully and without irony—perhaps because Rose is a dead dog—and because of all she learned about suffering during her short life.

But Cali—please—tell me what fucking kind of name is that for human being— even one from L.A.?

What was her mother thinking when she chose that name? But the less I think about what her mother—my ex-wife number three—thought or thinks the better. One thing I'm sure of though—she wasn't contemplating Kali, the dark Hindu goddess of undoing—when she named her daughter.

My ex-wife wouldn't know Kali if the goddess kicked her bony ass with her bare blue foot.

Cali's pupils fix me in their gaze, and then constrict into the impossible blue paleness of her eyes. "Charles," she screams, her bluish hand reaching for me. "Charles, help me!"

Chapter 3

"Three can keep a secret, if two of them are dead."

Benjamin Franklin

I drift toward Cali—my hand reaching for hers—but she disappears like vapor.

Rose floats over to the now acutely empty spot of nothingness that Cali briefly occupied, whines at the airless place, and looks at me questioningly.

I'm sure that a visit from Cali can only mean bad news.

How do I know this?

Two things.

The first—in life Cali only needed me when there was trouble.

And second—from what Rose and I have seen so far of death—only the dead can visit the dead.

Chapter 4

"But if death is the journey to another place, and there, as men say, all the dead are, what good, O my friends and judges, can be greater than this?"

Plato

I had stopped thinking about Cali long before I died.

And Cali's grotesque visit here reminds me of my death and of my life. The sensation of sunlight on skin, food and sex—love and friendship—regret and failure.

Seeing her makes me wonder if Rose and I have become—if this is possible—deader.

I look at my hands and my bare feet and they seem to have gone slightly grayish. Rose's reddish fur has faded a little, too—as if death is slowly, very slowly draining us of color. The bullet wounds in my neck and gut have blackened. My skin is dry.

But Cali looked freshly dead—or more accurately, maybe—recently alive, even with the blue tinge.

What a pain in the ass Cali could be—always getting in trouble. And fighting with her mother.

How can I possibly help her?

Here I don't have my wallet—which was fatter than even my royally fat ass—to fix things for her.

Here all I've got is Rose.

Chapter 5

"The key here, I think, is to not think of death as an end . . . think of it more as a very effective way of cutting down on your expenses."

Woody Allen

Since I found myself here in the afterlife with Rose, a few things about being dead have revealed themselves:

You do not—even in death—ever escape yourself.

What I was in life I remain. Thirty-eight year old fat man. Smart ass. Failure.

And Rose? Rose is the intelligent, patient and gentle dog she was in life.

What I knew and the ability to know persist.

But death—like life—imposes limitations.

On this side I can feel Rose's feathery fur against my fingers, can feel the pressure of her too-thin body against my leg.

On the other side Rose and I are less—much less.

We cannot touch the living—the living cannot touch us.

The living cannot see or hear us, either.

For all you know Rose and I—like x-rays—are passing right through your warm body right now.

Chapter 6

"Death fixes forever the relation existing between the departed spirit and the survivors upon earth."

John Quincy Adams

Rose and I float over a huge, round bed.

Cali's white-blond hair encircles her too-pale and less bluish face, and her head rests on the oversized square mauve satin pillow. The headboard is white leather with silver studs. It's night in your world and this room is ridiculous—as if Ozzy Osbourne decorated it himself.

"Is she breathing?" A red haired girl about Cali's age sits on the bed, oblivious to the ashes that fall from her cigarette onto the bedspread.

A boy in skinny jeans and a black t-shirt stands over Cali, then presses his ear close to her nose and mouth.

Rose—her eyes wide—moves close to Cali's face, too—as if she understands what this boy is doing and can feel—if Cali is breathing—any small puff of air that comes from her nose and mouth.

"Yeah. Look at her chest. It's moving up and down."

"But she looks dead!" the redhead whines, then slaps Cali's cheek hard.

Rose barks and I lurch forward to grab the girl, to shake her, to get her away from Cali, but my hands dissolve when they touch her living arm.

"Wake up, Cali!" she yells close to Cali's ear. "Wake up!"

Cali moans but doesn't open her eyes.

"We have to call 911!"

"Shut up. We're not calling anyone," black t-shirt says, turning his face toward the redhead. "Cali will be okay. I've seen people passed out lots of times."

Nice.

"But Zen," the girl persists.

His name is "Zen"?

"Zen" takes the fucking cake. Worst name ever. He must go to Cali's school.

"Cali looks horrible. And her fingers and toes were totally blue, didn't you see? Look." The girl lifts Cali's pale hand for Zen to look at. Cali's ring—an opal and a diamond on a slender gold band—sparkles in the candlelight.

"Shut up, Marissa. Just make sure she keeps breathing and doesn't vomit," Zen directs.

Marissa. At least that qualifies as a name. Marissa must go to another school, maybe a public magnet school for sociopaths.

Marissa tugs hard on Cali's the ring. Is she trying to steal it? Jesus.

But Cali's pale eyes flutter open and Marissa changes her mind and drops her hand.

Cali turns onto her side and vomits pale blue foam onto the bedspread.

Rose watches intently, hovering right next to Cali's face.

"Oh no! She's puking!" Marissa whines.

"That's good," Zen says and disappears into a large mirrored bathroom then returns with an embroidered towel. "That means the Klonopin is out of her stomach."

Klonopin. Too much of that can kill you. How much did Cali take? Was it Marissa's? Or did she get it from this boy?

"Don't use that towel!" Marissa whines. "It's my mom's. From France."

Towels from fucking France. Why am I surprised?

"Well go get some paper towels then," says Zen, who wipes Cali's mouth with the towel and then blots the bedspread.

"I can't," Marissa says, calm now, her eyes vague. "Consuelo will see me and will ask what happened and if I say I spilled something she'll want to come up here clean it up. And I don't want her to tell my parents we were in their room."

"I thought your parents were in San Francisco for the weekend," Zen says.

"They're flying back tonight."

"Tonight?" Zen repeats, exasperated. "Then we've got to get her the fuck out of here. Right now."

Chapter 7

"…often I felt [Death's] breath on my face when he was miles away; often I fell asleep and dreamed while he stood leaning over my bed."

Arthur Koestler

Zen pulls Cali off the large bed and drags her through large French windows onto a patio. He's so good at dragging an almost lifeless body that I suspect he's done it a few times before.

Marissa blows out the candles, grabs the soiled towel and smoothes the bed. She's about to run out the door when she turns back to pick up Cali's sandals and her large leather purse from the floor.

Cali's bare heels scrape the flagstone patio, then make two pale flat streaks in the damp grass in a huge moonlit back yard. Rose floats close to the grass—as if she's imagining how the moist green blades would feel beneath her paws.

Cali moans and her eyes open briefly, their orbs reflecting the moon's silver. I'm not sure where we are—but the flat expanse of grass and pool and now a tennis court— make me guess this is Encino or maybe Calabasas.

Zen drags Cali behind a guest house to a long and curving driveway, then stops near four cars parked in a row——a pale green Fiat, a Mini Cooper painted with a Union Jack design, a black Escalade, and an old Toyota. The Toyota must be Consuelo's.

Marissa is right below us now, carrying her oversized purse and Cali's bag and shoes. She rummages in Cali's bag and finds her car keys, then opens the door to the Mini Cooper and looks at Zen.

"How the fuck do I get her in?" he asks. "Bend her like a hanger? I hate Minis. Minis totally suck."

What a wag this asshole Zen is. He's right about one thing, though. Cali is limp—and very flexible.

"I'm cold, "Marissa whines. "And this is getting really boring. Can't we leave her on the street?"

Zen does not offer Marissa his jacket, but holds Cali and waits until Marissa drops the purses and the shoes and lifts Cali's muddy heels. Zen keeps his arms around Cali's chest. Rose has returned from the grass and floats right next to him.

"You first," he directs.

Marissa elbows the driver's seat down, pushes Cali's feet into the back and then releases her.

Zen pushes Cali—face first—into the tiny space, straightens, then leans in to lift her head.

"What about seatbelts?" Marissa asks.

"What about seatbelts?" Zen mocks.

Marissa lights a cigarette and looks at Cali stuffed sideways into the shallow back seat as if Cali were a piece of furniture they were donating to Goodwill.

"Yeah. I guess she's in there pretty tight. Maybe we should just drop her near an ER somewhere? Maybe one downtown or in Glendale?"

"Shut up and give me the keys," Zen says as he gets in the driver's seat. "You're not going anywhere. Go back in and make sure you bag up all the pills."

Chapter 8

"Death is progress, advance, disimprisonment."

Reuen Thomas

Rose and I join Cali in the impossibly small back seat of the Mini.

Being dead has advantages—we can stand on the heads of pins, squeeze into small spaces, and pass through walls, earth, and metal barriers.

Whenever the car moves under a light or when the road curves toward the full moon, I check Cali's chest and throat for a rise and fall that indicates respiration. She's breathing.

I was wrong—Marissa's house was in Agoura Hills. Zen takes Malibu Canyon south toward the beach—and traveling along the curving canyon road so fast that I am deeply grateful not to be alive. But Zen is relaxed as he smokes an electronic cigarette and listens to loud music—don't ask me what—everything he plays sounds like angry white men yelling.

Once we get to Pacific Coast Highway, Zen goes north, makes a U turn at Las Tunas Canyon beach and parks in a No Parking Anytime zone.

A jumble of dark rocks outlined in the moonlight leads to a narrow beach. Zen climbs out of the tiny car and scrambles down to the beach. Rose and I float through the Mini's back end into the night and watch him.

What the fuck can he be planning? To drown her?

Chapter 9

"It is only when caught in the swift, sudden turn of death, that mortals realise the silent, subtle, ever-present perils of life"

Herman Melville

Zen reappears on the side of the highway, frowns, and inhales deeply on his electronic cigarette. Then he walks to the Mini, opens the passenger door, and looks in at Cali. The little dome light goes on and he quickly closes the door again.

It's still dark—but it must be very late. Traffic is light on Pacific Coast Highway, but in the east the black sky is fades to blue.

Rose is nervous and stays close to me. She doesn't like the ocean and she avoids Zen. Rose is an expert on human cruelty and indifference—she spent her short life tied to a metal pole—frightened, hungry and thirsty.

How I know this is too long and strange a story to tell you now—except to say that death brought me to Rose—not the other way around—and that I've learned to respect her feelings.

A car approaches and slows, flashing its headlights. Zen waves and the car makes a U turn and parks behind Cali's car. I see that it's a green Prius. A tall, thin guy gets out. He's wearing flip-flops, khaki shorts and a white t-shirt.

"What kind of shit are you in now, Zen?" he asks, then opens the door of the Mini and looks at Cali. "Jesus. How stupid can you get? Who is she?"

"No one, Dylan." Zen says quietly, "We were at Marissa's house when she got, uh, sick."

Dylan shakes his head, then roughly pulls Cali's limp body out of the car and turns to Zen. "Get her purse and grab her feet."

Zen lifts Cali's bare feet and the two young men carry her over the rocks and then drop her on the damp sand. The tide is out, but not as far out now. How long before high tide returns?

"Stay here." Dylan scrambles over the rocks and opens the trunk of the Prius, then returns carrying a brown paper bag from which he removes a liquor bottle and unscrews the top—It's clear—maybe gin or vodka.

"Hold her head up." Zen lifts Cali's head as Dylan pushes the bottle's to her mouth and pours. The vodka makes Cali cough. The rest dribbles out of the corners of her mouth onto her shirt and pants.

"Don't choke her!" Zen says.

"Pour the rest on her clothes. Where's her wallet?" Zen fumbles with Cali's purse, then removes Cali's cell phone and her wallet. Dylan takes the credit cards and cash from the wallet and drops it on the sand. He runs to the water's edge and throws the cell phone into the roiling sea.

"It's almost light. Let's go."

Zen does not look back at Cali as he follows Dylan to the Prius, or when he gets inside.

Rose and I watch them drive away, then watch the waves. Each one moves closer to Cali than the last.

Chapter 10

"Whatever has a beginning must have an ending."

Francis Crick

When you die, they confiscate your watch. But Cali's been here enough for the sea to rise and for the tide to rhythmically deliver heavy, slate-colored waves.

Rose circles Cali's inert body anxiously, then looks into my eyes, her tail wagging with impatience.

Do something, Rose's tail and eyes admonish.

But I cannot pull Cali away from the encroaching waves.

I cannot shout for help.

And so I try to conjure an early-morning jogger, or a car that stalls—or better yet—a police car. I try to summon anyone alive to see what Rose and I see now—an unconscious seventeen-year-old girl about to be pulled into the sea.

Then Rose stops in mid-air like a hummingbird—her sensitive ears picking up a sound I cannot hear.

Now I make out the faint whine of sirens to the south. The sound swells until a red LAFD paramedic truck and a black and white turn and park along the rocky shoulder.

The paramedics exit the truck first, carrying metal boxes. They climb over the rocks to the narrowing, wet beach, then kneel alongside Cali's inert form.

Chapter 11

"Most of us were not afraid of death, only of the act of dying; and there were times when we overcame even this fear. At such moments we were free..."

Arthur Koestler

The Fire Department paramedics took Cali's vital signs, wrapped her in a silver blanket and carried her on a stretcher into the ambulance.

Now in the ER cubicle, Cali offers mumbled answers to the nurses' and doctor's questions.

Seventeen.
Klonopin.
I don't know.
Some.
Some Klonopin.
And weed.
And maybe some Valium.
No. No alcohol.
I said Klonopin.
No drinking.
Hallucinations?
Well I thought I saw my dead stepfather and a dead dog. Does that count?
Then Cali laughed.
What happened to my cell phone?

Rose hovers near Cali's narrow bed, and I float like a tethered helium balloon near Rose.

The cubicle curtains open.

Cali's mother—my ex-wife number three—and her contractor friend Steve walk right through me and Rose.

The clock on the wall says 7 A.M. but Elaine arrives in full makeup—false eyelashes, shiny clear lipstick, frosty eye shadow—and in high-heeled sandals and a silky blue dress. Her brown hair falls in soft curls around her face as if she visited her hairdresser on the way over. She looks good—if by good you mean she looks like an actress waiting to go on stage who wants her expressions to be visible to the people sitting near the rafters—and if by good you mean bee-stung lips and eyebrows frozen by Botox into permanently perplexed arches. She looks better than she did at my funeral, though. Tanner. Fitter. Thinner. As if she lives on a yacht instead of in that battlestar of a house she built in Beverly Fucking Hills.

"Oh God, Cali!" she yells. "Oh, God! My poor baby!" I assume this outburst is for Steve's benefit. Preppy Steve. Sunburned except for the white outline of sunglasses around his dark green eyes. Steve is dressed in a peach polo shirt—with the collar turned up—I hate that—and Topsiders without socks—I hate the no-sock thing, too. Right now his eyebrows knit in a look of concern—not for Cali—but because of something he's reading on his cell phone.

"I'm not a baby." Cali says clearly and loudly now, and I'm relieved.

Cali's okay. She's alert. Abrasive. Her brief demise and the overdose didn't damage her brain.

If I weren't already insubstantial, I'd feel as if a huge weight had been lifted from me.

"I just want to go home. Can you get me out of here, Elaine?"

Since I first met Cali when she was ten, Cali has addressed her mother by her first name. I thought then that this informality revealed something about Cali, but I know now that Elaine is so bereft of empathy and imagination that she is incapable of mothering.

"I spoke to the doctor. And to the hospital social worker. And to Mr. Christian," Elaine explains.

Mr. Christian is Elaine's lawyer.

"You're going to be released in a few hours. But—"

"But what?" Cali asks, suspicious.

"But you're not going home." Steve says this quickly, putting his arm tightly around Elaine's thin shoulders as if she—not Cali—were the one in trouble.

"From what we hear you could have died, Cali," Steve says sternly. "And that's not okay."

"Not okay"? If Steve only knew that Cali was really and truly dead—for a little while—what dumb-ass thing would he say then? "That's not nice"? Or "What a bummer?"

"Your life is out of control, Cali," Elaine says now, looking sad. "You keep getting high. And running away from home. From your responsibilities. And your problems."

Cali's eyes widen in surprise—then desperation. "Come on, Elaine. Please."

"You need treatment." Steve adds, his eyes narrowing. "And as your stepfather I'm telling you that out of love."

"Stepfather"? Elaine and Steve are married?

When the fuck did this happen?

You die and then nobody tells you a goddamn thing.

"And you will have this treatment where I've arranged to send you—" stepdad Steve continues in a stern faux-fatherly manner, "or in the county lock-up ward."

"You need help, Cali," Elaine adds. "And through one of his clients—whose son went there—Steve found a great treatment place near Santa Barbara. Casa des Girasoles. Steve heard it has gorgeous view of the beach. It's just like a 4 star hotel—"

Chapter 12

"Death lies dormant in each of us and will bloom in time."

Dean Koontz

Rose flinches with each shout.

I can't stand what I'm hearing, either.

Not because I'm vulnerable or sensitive. Because I've heard it all before.

Another moment spent listening to Elaine and Steve argue with Cali and I'll detonate like swamp gas.

Jesus.

Since the divorce and my murder, nothing—not one goddamn thing—has changed.

Cali is still infuriating.

Ditto for the unlovely former Mrs. Charles fucking Stone.

I barely knew Steve in life and I want to keep it that way. Once an asshole, always an asshole.

And because nothing is different—except that Steve and Elaine are married—I know exactly where this is heading and I refuse to go there with it—

Tears.

Threats.
Taunts.
Recriminations.
Provocations.
Ultimatum.

And then Cali will do whatever Steve and Elaine force her to do.

Until she turns eighteen she has no choice.

And maybe some time away from her fucked-up parents and her fucked-up friends might do Cali some good.

Cali asked for my help—and I did what I could—which in my current condition is nada—I know.

"We're finished here. " I say— trying to keep the bitterness out of my voice for Rose's sake. "Come on."

Chapter 13

"And nothing can we call our own but death..."

Shakespeare

Rose and I are back in death's unquiet hermitage—deep inside the thick silence that follows the final heartbeat, the last tortured breath.

Rose is stretched out in the airless space next to me, her chin resting on her paws, her eyes half-closed as she thinks her own serious thoughts.

Here's a heads-up for you—life haunts death—it's not the other way around. Cali's shitty friends, her overdose and Elaine's marriage to Steve—and Rose's suffering and the stupid way I died—shot on a street in Hollywood by a stranger—follow us here.

Having lived and died does not confer wisdom or inoculate one from regret—for what was done or what was not done—for what I knew or what I didn't know—for those I loved or failed in love.

You are thinking I should have been a better—what?

Stepfather?

Friend?

What a joke.

Cali and I were more like roommates than anything else in the huge house we shared when I was—for a short time—her mother's husband—one of a succession of stepfathers passing through Cali's life.

As if to demonstrate futility to me, Rose chases her own skinny tail in slow motion above my head.

It's the sort of charming dead canine thing that should make me almost smile.

But Elaine, Cali and Steve have disturbed my tomblike calm.

Shaken my equilibrium.

Made me question things I thought I knew for certain and thought I felt.

About myself.

And about other people, too.

Especially Cali.

Chapter 14

"And life is perfected by death."

Elizabeth Barrett Browning

The red tile-roofed buildings cluster below the hills south of Santa Barbara.

Rose likes the green lawns moist with fog—the bright red and purple geraniums—the riding paths and the stables, which house—in the eyes of a creature that has never seen a horse—some very large and very strange-looking dogs.

For once Elaine was right.

This place really is like a four-star hotel—except that you can't leave your room when you want to, can't phone out, can't have a computer, and can't own a belt or pair of shoes.

"I need to call my father!" A kid around fourteen yells to the silence inside his room in the high security wing of the Casa des Girasoles Center for Wellness and Recovery. "Do you fucking hear me?"

I'm outside the kid's room. His parents—the mother with huge pearls on her neck and ears, and wearing a wool pants suit—the slim, tall father in jeans and a black cashmere jacket over a white silk shirt.

With them is a man in a long white coat. The trio observes the boy on a black and white video monitor on the wall, and listens to an intercom switched to "ON."

The hallway floor is red-tiled and the walls are a homey and buttery yellow. Cheerful oil paintings of sunflowers appear at intervals in rustic wooden frames—I remember now that girasol means sunflower in Spanish—paintings of single tall sunflowers reaching skyward, fields of sunflowers dazzling yellow and green in the full noon light, blue vases of sunflowers on red-checked tablecloths—enough sunflowers to make you sick of sunflowers—even Van Gogh's—forever.

"David's reckless drug abuse is a form of acting out," the man in the white coat says, "and that, as we discussed earlier, is perfectly consistent with Oppositional Defiant Disorder. His irritability, his inability to make friends, his lack of respect for you both—everything you told me about are part of the ODD profile."

What teenager isn't "oppositional and defiant"?

Isn't something was wrong with them if they aren't?

David sounds a lot like Cali.

Maybe they'll become best friends.

Where is she? So far I haven't found her, but the place is large.

David's mother nods and when she does, large pearl drop earrings begin to swing back and forth. The father receives this diagnosis with a blank look.

The man in the white coat leans close to the intercom, then flips the switch and talks, "Good morning, David. Welcome to Casa des Girasoles. I'm Dr. Main and I'm going to take good care of you. There's nothing to be upset about.

Your mother and father are here. I'm talking with them right now and I want you to know that they love you very much."

Inside the small black and white screen the boy throws his pillow at the camera and yells, "Mom! Dad! Take me home. Please!"

David's parents are silent.

But it's the man in the white coat who throws me. David's agitation seems to make him almost happy.

David tosses another pillow at the camera, then pull the sheets off the bed and throw those, too.

The man switches off the intercom and turns to David's mother and father, "As I explained earlier, right now David can't evaluate himself, can't understand his own oppositional behaviors. Instead he mistakenly sees you and your husband as unreasonable."

"Our treatment plan for David here at Casa des Girasoles will allow him to see his own behaviors for what they are—oppositional and defiant. And we'll heal the source of his social isolation and his substance abuse—his low self esteem."

Oh no. Not that. Not low self fucking esteem.

Which by the way is a condition that has afflicted all if not most of the people who came near my father—kiddie TV star Happy Andy the Rodeo Clown—and all of Elaine's husbands.

Steve had better watch his ass.

David has stripped the bed and attempts to pull the lamp from the bedside table, but only the lampshade comes off. He throws that toward the camera, too.

"I need to get out of here! Listen to me! Please!"

"Yes, Dr. Main," Pearl earrings says and turns away from the monitor. "Self-esteem is everything, isn't it? Without that a person has nothing"

Bullshit.

David's father pats the pocket of his sport coat and removes a humming BlackBerry, then moves a few steps away to talk. His wife follows him down the hallway.

I can see Rose outside through the hall window behind him, floating in slow circles above a black horse being led out of the stables.

"Dad!" David yells, but I'm the only one watching or listening to him now— unless the goddamn sunflowers have ears.

Chapter 15

"Someone dying asks if there is life after death. Yes, comes the answer, only not yours."

E.L. Doctorow

I float through the sunflower-yellow wall and up above the rustic roofs.

Rose drifts away from the black horse and joins me as I scan the place.

A long honey-colored gravel driveway links Casa des Girasoles to a narrow canyon road that stretches a mile until it meets a wrought iron gate. Past the gate, a narrow frontage road curves south toward Carpinteria.

Fog mutes the early morning sounds and obscures the hills, the eucalyptus trees, and beyond them the 101 Freeway and beyond that, the sea.

I imagine that on a clear day a patient at Casa des Girasoles could see Anacapa Island's outline across the Santa Barbara Channel. But now the sun is just a dull white smudge.

I drift over the main building, then above the four smaller residential "casitas" that encircle an enclosed courtyard, and behind those, the wooden roofed stables, the tennis court, a large swimming pool and the wood-roofed outdoor ceramics studio.

I see a few kids walking toward the stables. I drift down close to their heads—no Cali.

Rose and I move to the main building and pass through the large wooden entrance door carved with sunflowers. The empty reception area is airy, with overstuffed brown leather sofas arranged around a large stone fireplace and floor-to- ceiling windows revealing a garden. At the front there is a desk equipped with a set of monitors and telephones, and a door behind that painted the same yellow as the walls which are adorned with rustic paintings of—you guessed it—sunflowers.

I move close to a framed document hanging over the fireplace, the borders of which are decorated with clip-art images of sunflowers and whose text is printed in an ugly and curly font: Reach for the Sun! Stand Tall! Love Yourself! Have the Courage to Leave the Past Behind! Try Something New! Learn! Embrace Your Future! Work Hard!

Casa des Girasoles must be the second fucking happiest place on earth, and right now it's the quietest. A deathly quiet—and I mean deathly—fills this place. Are all the windows soundproofed?

Although the place has a cozy, rustic vibe, the more I look, the more high-tech monitoring devices are visible. The bulging black eyes of video cameras peer from behind the leaves of potted plants in the roughly woven baskets on side tables. Video cameras that look like dark round light fixtures are mounted on the ceilings and above the entrance and the yellow door behind the desk. There must be microphones, but I'm not sure where they are.

Rose's ears swivel toward the reception desk. Her eyes widen.

Chapter 16

Rose drifts to a yellow door behind the reception desk. Now I see what Rose wanted me to notice—near it is a lighted electronic keypad that requires a numerical code to open it.

Rose melts right through the door, and I follow her into a short and narrow windowless hallway illuminated by greenish fluorescent lights.

There are no cheerful yellow walls, no plants, and not even one sunflower here. A mustached middle-aged man in mustard-yellow scrubs sits at a desk across from a computer whose flickering black and white images reveal patients asleep in their beds, the empty reception area, and a dining room in which a janitor mops the wooden floor.

Next to the man is what looks like a small nurses' station complete with patient files in clear Plexiglas holders, carts with medical equipment, and three more desktop computers.

"How did the night go?" A thick middle-aged woman with very short black hair enters through the reception area door. She also wears yellow scrubs and carries a large purse and a thermal lunch bag.

This must be a shift change—he's night and she's day.

"Same as last night," the man says, then stands and stretches. "There's a new one. Substance abuse. Depression. Hallucination. ODD. The usual. Paul wants her intake done right after breakfast. "

The new one could be Cali. I turn to go but Rose stays where she is, intently watching the man hand the woman a file folder.

The woman glances at it, and then appears annoyed. "Why didn't you do her intake, Justin? She was admitted on your shift, right? And you know that Mondays are my busiest day because of the weekly status reports." The woman opens a drawer and shoves her lunch bag and purse inside, then slams it shut and attaches a small two-way radio to a clip on her hip pocket.

Rose's ears perk up. She growls.

What is it? What is bothering her?

"I'm sorry, April. We had trouble with that kid in 112 after bed check. José found him smearing his shit all over the walls and it took three of us to restrain him. He's been having some alone time in the happy room. It's up to you when he gets out."

Justin types something on his keyboard and a grainy black and white surveillance image of a boy hog-tied and lying face down on a hospital gurney fills the screen.

There is no sound except April's cruel laugh and another low growl from Rose.

Jesus.

Reaching for the sun, my ass.

Chapter 17

"...it is well for us, now and then, to talk with death as friend talketh with friend..."

Henry Ward Beecher

The fog has burned off. Casa des Girasoles is full of jaundiced light. And as if they didn't have enough of them already, the receptionist arranges fresh sunflowers in a large blue vase and puts it on the mantle over the fireplace.

Rose hangs impatiently behind me in the air as I try to locate the hog-tied boy and the happy room. Once I do that, I will find Cali and—somehow—get her the fuck out of here.

I find Dr. Paul Main's office, just a few doors past the large dining/meeting room with its ping pong table and pool table along one wall, its homey shelves cluttered with board games and books. Dr. Main's office has a large oak desk, three leather chairs opposite it—for family meetings, I imagine—and a nice view of the swimming pool. His walls are covered with framed pictures of himself smiling at smiling teens, with people wearing scrubs, of himself in jeans riding a horse, and with a brown-haired woman and twin toddler boys at the beach. I look for diplomas--most doctors have them prominently displayed—but all I see is a Santa Barbara Chamber of Commerce award from 2010.

Rose and I return to the reception area.

I'm not sure where to look.

But Rose doesn't stop. She passes once again through the yellow security door. April sits playing an online poker game on the computer.

What if they are keeping Cali back here, too?

We advance, first Rose, then me, right through April's stocky form.

We float through a metal door into an empty room.

Gray walls, a gurney in the middle, and not much else except a sink, a locked cupboard, and in the corner a metal cart holding an assortment of thick white and black restraints.

Then a shower room, a restroom, and a locked pharmaceutical cupboard.

Then Rose floats through the only door that's left—a narrow metal door that looks like the door to a small janitorial supply closet.

Chapter 18

*"I shall soon be laid in the quiet grave--thank God for the quiet grave--
O! I can feel the cold earth upon me--the daisies growing over me--O for
this quiet--it will be my first."*

*Attributed to John Keats in a letter from Joseph Severn to John Taylor,
Mar. 6, 1821*

I follow Rose through the narrow metal door.

There he is.

Rose becomes wild-eyed and barks above the boy--still
hog-tied and face down on the black gurney.

Rose knows what it's like to be tied up and left alone.

I move close to the boy's face—snot bubbles from his
nostrils—he's breathing.   But his hands and bare feet—
bound by the tight Velcro restraints—are white.

How old is he? Thirteen? He's slight—and because he's
only wearing boxers—I can see that he's thin and almost
hairless.

Shit. He's a child.

The narrow door opens and April angles her wide self
through followed by two men who look more like gardeners
than medical staff in their dark green uniforms.

"How are we feeling this morning?" April asks.

The boy moans. The two men stand silently behind
April.

"How are we feeling this morning?'" April repeats.

The boy tries to turn his head toward her, but can't and moans again.

"That's better," April says. "Rule two at the Casa is that you speak when spoken to."

The boy is quiet but I can see that he is trembling.

"You know what rule one is?" April leans down and yells into the boy's ear.

The boy struggles against the restraints.

"Rule one is we don't smear crap around our rooms. You got that, Ethan? You worthless piece of shit. "

So much for Ethan's self-esteem.

Rose moves away from Ethan and April and cowers behind me.

April nods at the two men. They release Ethan from the restraints and then roughly pull him off the gurney. Ethan is so wobbly that his legs give out.

"José and Richard are going to help you wake up with a nice cold shower. Then they'll give you supplies that you will use to clean your room, floor to ceiling. And then, if I decide that your room is spotless, you will get something to eat. Understood?"

Ethan's only answer is the glob of mucus he spits toward April as the two men drag him out the door and into the shower room.

Chapter 19

"Life is hard, but death is even harder."

Peter Kreeft

Aprils gathers a clipboard, papers and a pen, and the file Justin had given her and moves through the security door into the sunlit reception area. I follow April and a frightened Rose follows me, her big eyes downcast, her tail between her legs.

April pauses to chat with the young woman behind the desk, then walks past the overstuffed leather couches on which two nervous and unhappy parents and a sullen teenaged boy with nose and cheek piercings sit with Dr. Main.

When Dr. Main sees April, he pats the teenager on the shoulder and stands to go. "It was great meeting you, Greg. And Mr. and Mrs. Gould, we'll be talking more this afternoon."

We follow Dr. Main and April and through another door that leads to the yellow hallway.

"This is the new patient. Cali Green," Dr. Main says. "Nothing unusual in her intake that I could see."

April nods as she enters an eight-digit code in the numerical keypad on the door.

But before the door opens, Rose and I pass through it and enter.

An unmade bed sits primly inside the empty room.

Chapter 20

"Death is only a small interruption."

Anita Brookner

Where is she?

I float through the door leading to a windowless, lock-less en-suite bathroom—a towel has been thrown on the floor—the only indication that Cali was ever here.

Back in the room, April is on all floors looking under the bed.

She shakes her head "no" at Dr. Main, whose face tightens into a scowl, then groans as if her back hurts as she gets to her feet.

Dr. Main touches a button on the wall and speaks curtly. "José. Richard. Justin. We've got a missing flower arrangement in Casita Number 3. I repeat. We have a missing flower arrangement in Casita Number 3. The flowers are pink."

Dr. Main releases the button. "This breakaway is completely unacceptable. And I hold you responsible, April. You are the senior aide on this shift. What the hell have you been doing instead of monitoring the video cameras for this wing?"

Before April can think of anything to say, Dr. Main turns quickly and exits the room, the bottom of crisp, white coat tails rising behind him.

Chapter 21

"Death is real. Death changes things. Everything else is merely a message from our sponsor."

Michael Marshall

Rose and I drift from room to room in Casa des Girasoles, but we do not find Cali.

As we search for her I cannot stop myself from remembering my life with Cali and Elaine.

How I hated attending the LA Philharmonic fundraisers, LA Zen Collective fundraisers, political fundraisers, feminist fundraisers and every event or committee meeting or show or sale or concert at Cali's school—auctions, fairs, theater productions, teacher appreciation luncheons, holiday sales, meetings with the board of trustees and the hellish annual circle dinner with the headmistress.

How I hated working with—or I should say "under"— my shit brother Mark at the family business, AndyCo.

How I hated coming home to find Elaine dressed up and ready to go out.

As we'd leave Elaine would call to Cali where she sat on one of the oversized silk upholstered dining room chairs with one of the tutors Elaine had hired to make her do her homework.

Or to do her homework for her.

Or on our way out we'd pass Cali coming in the door—with a nanny or a babysitter who drove her to modern dance, to martial arts, or tennis, or to her psychiatrist, or from getting her eyebrows, legs and forearms waxed.

Even on those rare occasions when I picked up Cali after school, I barely spoke to her except to ask, "Do you want something at Starbucks or at Jamba Juice?"

Cali would briefly remove an earbud from her ear or pause her texting to say, "Yeah."

Well Cali's gotten herself into serious trouble now. In more danger than she knows.

Chapter 22

"Thus am I doubly armed: my death and life,
My bane and antidote, are both before me..."

Joseph Addison

It's late afternoon in your world.

Richard, Jose and Justin are doing no better than we are in their search for the missing floral arrangement—pink—a.k.a. Cali Green.

We follow them into the dining room where kids receive medication from April in a plastic cups.

We float near them as they do a bed check, a room check, a grounds check.

Then we drift above them into the ceramics studio, a shed filled with identical little clay bowls waiting to be fired in the kiln.

Now we sail above the three men as they sit astride horses—one a gleaming chestnut brown, the other two dappled black and gray—on the riding trail that edges the property.

One of the men I saw in the happy room with David--José or Richard—speaks: "Let's check the path and then circle back."

The other men nod. One takes a pack of cigarettes from his pocket, lights one and begins to smoke.

The other takes out his cell phone with one hand, keeping his other hand lightly on the reins.

The man in front urges his horse to quicken its pace, then makes a clicking noise and calls over his shoulder to the two horses behind him, "Sunflower, Sundance, hurry up!"

The horses break into a gentle trot. They proceed on the empty path until—I'll choose one name—José—because it fits the Casa des Girasoles bullshit Spanish theme—pulls the reins and stops.

A sharp and rocky incline descends below the path about fifty feet to a tall chain link fence overgrown in places with cobalt morning glories. Beyond the fence are steep hills, a citrus or avocado grove, then the glowing sun and reflective sea.

The three men stare through the fence for a little while—scanning for Cali.

"We're not going to find her," José says finally. "I think that puta April forgot to lock the room. The girl could have made it down the driveway before we even knew she was gone."

The men receive this information without emotion or surprise.

The eastern edge of the sky is darkens like a bruise and the disappearing sun sends sharp, orange beams of last light across the horses and the men.

José clicks and the horses move forward, quickening their pace as they head toward the stables.

Then José's horse stumbles on a rut.

José leans down and says, "Cálmate" into its ear.

As he leans forward, something sparkles against his shirt.

I glide down close to him and before José can tuck it back inside his shirt I see a gold cross—and with it on a thick gold chain glitters Cali's opal ring.

Chapter 23

"Must not all things at the last be swallowed up in death?"

Plato

Did José take her ring?

Or did Cali use it to buy her freedom?

How far could she get without a phone or cash?

As the three men guide their horses into the stables, Rose rises over the steep hill toward the sea.

She stares seaward, then turns and looks meaningfully at me.

I look where Rose looks.

Another fence, then an avocado grove, some tract-style houses and a frontage road with street lights every two hundred feet or so.

Nothing.

Maybe she saw a bird. Or a squirrel.

Rose whines, insistent.

I look again.

A slender female figure runs from the shadows into an oval pool of light below a streetlamp.

Chapter 24

"...to die is different from what any one supposed, and luckier."

Walt Whitman

Rose reaches Cali first.

She lingers close to Cali's head, her feathery tail wagging.

Cali's chest heaves and her cheeks are red, but she doesn't stop running until she reaches the entrance to Highway 101 North.

It's dark now. The cars on the highway have their headlights on. But this freeway entrance and the frontage road that leads to it is empty.

Cali stays where she is until a black pickup truck turns onto the on-ramp and slows to a stop.

"Please!" Cali shouts, waving, and jumping up and down. "I need a ride!"

Chapter 25

"Death has a hundred hands and walks by a thousand ways."

T.S. Eliot, Murder in the Cathedral

The pickup stops.

If it were beating, my heart would stop as Cali opens the passenger door and climbs in.

Rose and I melt through the steel door after her.

The interior lights reveal a thirtyish guy with scraggly reddish beard and moustache. His head his shaved and he wears jeans, work boots and a gray sweatshirt with the sleeves ripped off to reveal freckled and muscular arms. He watches intently as Cali climbs quickly into the cab and shuts the door.

"Thank you!" Cali says, breathless. "I really needed a ride."

Left hand on the wheel, man rummages around the cluttered interior with his right. There are papers, a large metal thermos, empty beer bottles, chip bags and fast food wrappers. He locates a pack of Marlboros and tilts it toward Cali, but she shakes her head. He looks into the rear view mirror and drives back onto the freeway entrance ramp.

I hear the door locks click.

Rose hates this guy. She keeps her insubstantial and invisible self near Cali, but she keeps her big, wary eyes on the man.

I don't like him either. Or his truck and its tinted windows.

Shit. Why couldn't Cali have walked along the side of the freeway until she found an emergency telephone?

"No problem," he says, staring at her chest. "Where you going?"

"Where are we?" Cali asks. "I need to get back to LA, but if you're not going that way, then that's okay. I just need to get as far away from here as possible."

"You in some kind of trouble?"

"Sort of." Cali says, then corrects herself, "Not really. Just a misunderstanding. It's kind of complicated."

"Ain't it always?" the man laughs.

He doesn't introduce himself or ask Cali her name. Bad sign. And he doesn't tell Cali where he is going. Why not?

The traffic is light and the man moves the truck into the fast lane and speeds up, then rummages on the cluttered dashboard and finds a joint.

"Mind?" he asks Cali as he lights it with the dashboard lighter.

"No, that's fine," Cali says. "Where did you say you were going?"

"I didn't," he says, and inhales deeply, then holds the smoke in his lungs for a few seconds before exhaling slowly. "This is good shit. You should really have some. You seem really uptight."

Cali shakes her head and slides as far away from the man as she can on the bench seat, then looks at her reflection in the dark window.

Good. Stay alert, Cali. Stay alert.

The man smokes and drives north toward Santa Barbara. "You have a fight with your boyfriend?" he asks.

"I don't have a boyfriend," Cali says, her right hand on the side of the handle of the door. "And you can drop me off here. I'd like to get out now."

The man reaches for Cali's left arm with his right hand, keeping his left on the steering wheel, but Cali pulls away. "Come on. I'm sure you have a boyfriend. Maybe more than one."

Rose barks, a sharp, loud warning that neither Cali nor the man can hear.

Cali pulls her arm away, and is very quiet as the truck passes the exits for downtown Santa Barbara.

"You know. The best way to get revenge is to make your boyfriend jealous." The man grabs Cali's arm again, but this time, his grip is tight.

"Stop it!" Cali says. "Please. Just let me go. Let me get out right here."

The man laughs. "I don't think so. Not yet."

Cali attempts to open the truck door with her free hand, but she can't unlock it. Now she turns, trying to force the man to relinquish his hold. Cali keeps wriggling and struggling against his grip, then wrenches herself around, twisting the man's wrist as she does.

The moment his grip weakens, Cali lunges for the steering wheel and forces the car sharply to the right.

"Hey!" the man says, angry now, and slaps her away. "Are you trying to kill us, bitch?"

Rose barks uselessly at the man.

The man straightens the truck and speeds off the freeway at an exit marked SANTA BARBARA AIRPORT/UCSB. He drives the long straightaway at sixty, maybe seventy miles an hour—all the time holding Cali's forearm tightly.

Cali is so still that I'm afraid she's given up. But as the truck slows to take the sharp turn marked Sandspit Road, she grabs the large metal thermos and slams it against the side of the man's head.

The thermos must be full—it meets his forehead and cheekbone with a heavy thud.

Rose whimpers and flattens her ears.

"You fucking bitch!" Blood pours down his face from a large gash in his eyebrow. One hand on the wheel, he lets go of Cali's arm to wipe the blood from his eye.

Cali sees her chance. Both hands on the thermos now, Cali hits his head at the hairline again with the thermos.

Rose cowers.

Bloody gashes appear on the man's head, and blood pours down his face, reddening his beard and dripping onto his sweatshirt. He makes a guttural sound and Cali hits him again and again until he relinquishes his grip on the steering wheel and slumps against the blood-spattered window.

Fuck.

Did she kill him? Did Cali just kill this man?

Cali drops the thermos, grabs the steering wheel and maneuvers the bouncing truck to the side of the narrow road surrounded by what looks like a swamp.

But Cali can't reach the brake pedal. The truck keeps moving.

Pull out the key! I yell, but she can't hear me.

Cali pulls hard on the emergency brake. The truck slows, but doesn't stop. Cali looks around wildly then grabs the key from the ignition.

The truck bounces across a ditch, slows and stops.

The man groans as Cali reaches across his limp body to unlock the doors. She grunts as she pushes the man out the door into the ditch where he lands in some brush with a soft dull sound. Cali grabs the bloody thermos, hops out of the truck, and runs through the darkness toward the swamp.

Cali throws the thermos as far as she can and waits until she hears a splash before running back to the truck.

Cali slams the door shut, locks the doors and starts the engine. She maneuvers the truck out of the ditch, then drives fast down the dark and curving road.

Chapter 26

"So they pass away: friends, kindred, the dearest-loved, grown people,
aged, infants..."

William Makepeace Thackeray

Cali drives the truck past a car rental return and then past the Santa Barbara Airport entrance. She turns right on Hollister Avenue and keeps going until she reaches the sharp, curving on-ramp to Highway 101 South. Tears run down her cheeks and she takes in huge gulps of air through her mouth.

Calm now, Rose rests just above the front seat, her head above Cali's thigh.

What about the man? He was groaning when Cali pushed him out of the truck —how long before he comes to? And what if he doesn't?

And what will Cali do? Will she have the sense to get rid of the truck as soon as she can?

Cali drives south toward L.A.—sometimes at the speed limit, sometimes faster, but mostly she keeps up with thin traffic on the road at this hour—the clock on the truck dashboard says 11 P.M.

I'm surprised—Cali is a good driver—focused and alert. She pushes through Ventura, then Oxnard, then Camarillo, then takes the steep and winding hill to Thousand Oaks in the middle lane.

But as the truck's tires meet the top of the steep grade, two Ventura County sheriff's cars emerge from the dark entrance to the closed Weigh Station and flank the truck, red and blue lights spinning and sirens sounding. Then a third black and white appears and cuts in front of Cali.

"Shit!" Cali says as the cruisers manoeuvre the truck toward the shoulder.

The sheriff's cars hiss to a stop in the loose gravel, and the car doors fly open. Uniformed officers kneel behind the open doors and aim their handguns at Cali.

"Open the door slowly and put your hands up!"

Chapter 27

"Death is the mother of beauty."

Wallace Stevens

Death may be minimalist—but it is rich with irony.

I have returned to the house I promised—"over my dead body"—never to enter again—and in the place I detest more than any other on the living earth—Beverly Fucking Hills.

The only solace is the lawn—Rose loves its long and gentle slope, the trim borders and its perfect green. She skims its surface like a hawk on a warm updraft.

Elaine created this neo-Georgian red-bricked, white-columned, three-storied, six-car-garaged, circular drivewayed, triple-fountained, twin-tennis-courted, guest housed, ten bathroomed, bideted, saunaed, spinning gymed, grand staircased, butler pantried, Sub-zeroed, triple Viking ranged, wine-cellared, home theatered and libraried architectural abortion with the help of my very generous divorce settlement—which was worth every penny—and a "contractor to the stars" whom she was fucking before and during our brief union.

This house is so goddamned big, its bricks so fucking red, its grass so fucking emerald green, its wine room so fucking perfectly temperature-controlled, that it almost satisfies Elaine's appetite for the grandiose.

Here's another irony: The living think purgatory— if it exists at all—comes after life. Well, wrong again—marriage is purgatory—that's what I've found out.

I know. You're wondering what Elaine saw in me. Or why I married her. Yeah. So am I.

If it's any defense, I was on the rebound after a breakup so painful that my heart was frozen numb. And though love failed me—or I failed love--nonsensically I thought the best thing to do was to start the whole fucking romance thing again.

Also I was a lot more appealing when I was alive—for one thing, I had shoes. And then there was my money.

And after Elaine factored in the money—which really wasn't mine at all when you consider that it came from the family business, AndyCo.—which was built on my father's talents—I must have been almost attractive. Did I mention my father was the famous and miserable Happy Andy Cowboy Rodeo Clown and star of a 1960's and 70's children's television show?

But it is Cali who brings me here with Rose—not Elaine.

Cali—the teen goddess of sullenness, eye makeup, pharmaceutical over-intoxication, running away, bad luck—and, I see now—courage.

After Cali's arrest for assault and for stealing the truck—did it really require six armed uniformed officers and two helicopters to arrest a frightened teenager?—she was booked at the Thousand Oaks station where she made a phone call to her mother, then was transported to the Santa Barbara Jail where Steve and her lawyer Christian paid her bail and drove her—excuse the expression—home.

Chapter 28

No part of Elaine's house is more pretentious, excessive, grandiose, self-promoting, shiny, sterile, pompous, showy, useless, unnecessarily complicated, oppositional or defiant than this kitchen.

A small, primitive village could inhabit it comfortably including its ancient cemetery, its massive shit pile and its herds of goats.

An enormous antique crystal chandelier glitters smugly above the distressed wood of a French country farm table — presumably purchased directly from distressed French farmers who smothered it in bubble wrap before they shipped it here. Everywhere the expensive and glossy surfaces whisper, "I cost more money than you probably make in a year"—the warm mahogany, the chilly marble, the cool glow of stainless steel—satiny drapes the color of pomegranates, or as Elaine would call them—"window treatments"—the china, the silver, the restaurant stove and high-end appliances, the pot filler, the induction oven and even the warming drawer which the housekeeper is opening right now to reveal croissants Elaine will never ever eat.

The middle-aged and overweight housekeeper wears a pale pink uniform with starched appliance-white collar. The sleeves dig into the soft flesh of her wide, soft upper arms, as she removes croissants with silver tongs and arranges them on a porcelain plate with flowers on it—as if she is making a morning pick-me-up for the Queen of England instead of for Elaine, Steve, Cali, and the lawyer Christian—in a shiny gray suit and a Harvard crimson bow tie with little gold Harvard crests on it.

Be honest. How many Harvard graduates do you know who are even barely tolerable? And how many men who wear bow ties can you stand to be around?

In front of Christian and his bowtie on the French farmhouse table is a pile of papers, color brochures that have photos of rocks and pine trees on them, a BlackBerry, and an iPad in a leather case.

"Steve and I really appreciate your meeting with us on a weekend," Elaine says.

The lady of the house sits at her expensive farmer's table, a delicate gold-rimmed demitasse of espresso in front of her—her nail polish is almost the same color as the curtains. Steve drinks Starbucks from a cardboard to-go cup and wears his running clothes—black shorts and a green t-shirt that says "Beverly Hills Buddhism Center "as if Beverly Hills and Buddhism weren't an oxymoron—and the moment the word Buddhism mixes with the word Beverly Hills, Buddhism will instantly combust.

Poof.

Where's the Buddha when you need his detachment the most?

Dead with his fucking gingko tree.

Stuck somewhere in the afterlife not of his own choosing—just like me and Rose.

The Buddha could be floating alone and looking inward, I suppose—or—although I cannot see him—in his own dead universe detachedly observing Rose float like the Cheshire cat in the orange tree heavy with fruit outside the kitchen window.

How the fuck would I even know?

Death—not life—is the mystery.

Cali sits on a high stool at the long marble counter. She uses an ornate silver butter knife to flatten sticky globs of Nutella on a croissant and then takes a swig of Coca Cola from the can. She's wearing flannel pajama pants, Ugg boots and a neon green spaghetti strap t-shirt.

"As I explained in the District Attorney's office yesterday, I'm happy to do anything I can to help," Christian says, looking in Cali's direction. "And I think the best way to approach this problem is to view it as an opportunity."

Cali slathers Nutella on her second croissant. "You know," she says to the housekeeper—not to the man, "I love Nutella more than anything in the world. I'm going to change my name to Nutella. It sounds like a girl's name, doesn't it? And now that I've been locked up in an insane asylum, it's perfect. Nutella Williams Green Cansler plus the name of whichever guy marries my mother next."

Elaine's surgically lifted face tightens in anger.

"Turn around," Elaine says.

"You heard her," Steve hisses.

Cali turns slowly to face them.

"Mr. Christian is here to help you, Cali," Steve says through his clenched and blindingly whitened teeth. "Listen to him. If you don't, you'll end up in Juvenile Hall. Which. Is. Jail." Steve speaks in staccato for effect. "He doesn't have time for your bullshit. And your mother and I don't, either."

Christian adjusts his Harvard bowtie and smiles. He's smooth. Very smooth, maybe because each excruciating sad minute that uses itself up means fifty bucks in his well-tailored pocket. "Cali," he says evenly. "Assaulting someone and stealing a vehicle are extremely serious offenses. Even for a minor."

"I told you," Cali shouts, "that creep was kidnapping me! Trying to rape me! I hit him to defend myself. Why isn't he in trouble?"

"Mr. Smith is recovering from a serious head injury," Christian says patiently. "And at present he has no memory of giving you a ride or driving you to Santa Barbara."

"He's lying! Why do you believe him and not me? You don't believe me! Why don't you believe me?" Cali begins to sob. "Why?"

"You ran away from Casa des Girasoles," Steve yells. "Maybe Mr. Christian is wondering about your capacity for self-control."

Steve's voice draws Rose from the tree and through the glass window to Cali's side.

The enormous kitchen is silent except for the whisper of the German dishwasher and the sound of the plate Cali throws in Steve's direction shattering against the wall.

The housekeeper quickly begins to sweep up the pieces of broken porcelain.

Christian smiles and resumes as if nothing happened, "What occurred that night—or what didn't occur—doesn't matter right now, Cali." He pauses for emphasis. "What matters now is your future."

Why can't he say that he believes her?

Why can't Elaine or Steve say it? The running away was stupid. But do they really think she'd steal a truck and beat a strange man about the head for fun?

"Steve and I love you very much, Cali," Elaine says as if in response to an invisible cue from a community theater director offstage. Then she dabs her eyes with her cloth napkin, avoiding the mascara. "Please, listen to Mr. Christian. For your own good. "

"Cali," the lawyer continues. "Because you've received a psychiatric diagnosis of O.D.D. and other mental illnesses, at the arraignment yesterday I was able to convince the prosecutor to opt for informal probation. What this means is that if you comply with the conditions agreed upon—that you immediately complete a full—" He lets "complete" sink in— "course of residential treatment—the petition against you will be dismissed."

Chapter 29

Dying is an art.
Like everything else…

Sylvia Plath

The female mastodon and her calf are frozen in panic beneath the starless night sky. Their raised trunks point to the massive curving, upward pointing tusks of a male—his huge open mouth about to release a bellow of fear as the pool of black asphalt swallows his massive form.

Cali, Marissa and Zen observe this tableau from the Wilshire Boulevard side of the fence enclosing the La Brea Tar Pits—all is quiet except for a scattering of late night traffic and the bubbles of methane that occasionally rupture the oily surface.

Rose is beyond the far side of the fence, a shade spiraling down the steep green hill next to the Page Museum, then reversing direction and floating back up.

But much more is wrong here than Rose's post-mortal exemption from the law of gravity.

The really fucked up thing is not this pool of tar in which one diminutive human skeleton—a 38,000 year old homicide victim known as La Brea Woman—was among the million bones belonging to thirsty and unlucky animals who died here by suffocation, drowning or predation.

The really fucked up thing is not the red satin right shoe belonging to a pair of Elaine's wildly expensive high heels that Cali removes from her big leather bag and throws over the fence into the pool where it catches on a sticky pile of twigs and joins the dying concrete mastodon in the late Pleistocene stew of saber-toothed tigers and dire wolf bones.

No. The really not good, fucked up thing is that Cali— her pale eyes carefully made up, her lips shiny with pale lip gloss, her jeans skinny, her boots thigh-high—has sneaked out of Elaine's house where she is—according to Mr. Christian—on house arrest—to come here with the spectacularly disagreeable and slimy Marissa and Zen.

"I hate the way this place smells like rotten eggs," Marissa whines. "I hate the bones. I hated having to come here on elementary school on field trips."

"It sucks," Zen says. "Literally."

Zen is so fucking self-satisfied I'd like to throw him in.

"Maybe the shoe will make someone think Elaine threw herself into the tar." Cali says. "You know, that she killed herself because her daughter is a criminal. And because she's such a failure as a mother."

"You can always hope," Zen says.

"Yeah," Marissa says. "Didn't you just steal her shoe? That's a crime. And throwing it into the tar pits has to be against the law."

Cali laughs.

Zen lights a cigarette and smiles as a thought occurs to him. "Why don't you go in after it?"

Marissa's eyes widen for a moment and then she grins. "Yeah, why don't you jump in? That would really freak out Elaine and Steve, don't you think?"

"And you have nothing to lose." Zen says. "You're already in deep shit, aren't you?"

"Very funny," Cali says, bluster in her voice. "I thought we were going to Canter's."

"I'm not hungry anymore." Zen says.

"Me neither," Marissa agrees. "This stench makes me feel like throwing up."

"I dare you," Zen says. "Just dip your foot in the tar. We can hoist you over the fence. No problem."

"Yeah. And how would I get out?" Cali asks. "Come on. Let's go." Cali starts to walk east on Wilshire.

"Wait!" Zen shouts. "How about making it look like you jumped in? Give me your clothes."

Rose sails away from the lawn and drifts close to Cali. Her nostrils—which unfortunately can no longer detect or enjoy the delicious and varied smells of asphalt, smog, and stink of slow decay that floats inside cool night air—flare in alarm.

"Come on" Marissa says, and trots to Cali and then pulls Cali's large leather bag from her arm. "It would be so hilarious."

"Give it back to me," Cali yells, trying to grab the purse. "It's bad enough that I sneaked out tonight. Getting caught trespassing would just be too much right now." Cali catches her breath. "Please. Give me back my purse."

"You're such a stupid bitch," Marissa says, flushing with anger. "You really are. You're fucking pathetic."

"She's right," Zen says. "You are truly stupid and pathetic."

Marissa throws Cali's purse high over the fence.

She has a good arm.

The purse sails over the mastodon calf, the long straps just missing getting caught on one upturned tusk, then drops with a heavy plop upside down into the black and bubbling asphalt.

Chapter 30

Look out, Death: I am coming…

Sidney Lanier

I am not Cali's fairy fucking stepfather.

I cannot spirit her back to Beverly Hills—or levitate her purse from the pit of tar.

All I can do is watch Cali hug herself as she stands alone and watches her purse sink slow-motion into the ooze, then dig her brand new cell phone out of her jeans' pocket and dial a number.

"Gloria? Esta Cali. Si." Cali whispers.

"Por favor, don't let Elaine or Steve know you're talking to me, okay? Si. Please. I need a favor. Can you pick me up? I'll be at Fairfax and Wilshire."

"Please! Gloria. I can't pay for a taxi. I lost my wallet. What about Roberto?"

Gloria says something I can't make out.

"Gracias, Gloria," Cali says quietly. "Gracias."

Chapter 31

"And as life is to the living, so death is to the dead."

Mary Mapes Dodge

Cali clicks off her cell phone, pushes it back into the pocket of her jeans, and walks past the high fence enclosing the tar pools and then past the Museum of Art with its Chris Burden installation of street lamps, the ugly, boxy Broad building, the former May Company building, then crosses the street at Fairfax.

Cali stops at the corner in front of the blue and white striped Johnie's Coffee Shop Restaurant.

Cali's eyes scan the blur of cars on Wilshire. Rose has leapt up above the top of the box and hovers there with her legs curled under her like a deer. In solidarity with Cali, Rose looks at the cars, too.

It is that time of night when sounds intensify, shadows deepen, when the living world seems insubstantial—like a movie set about to be struck and a new fake city erected in its place.

Cali pulls her thin sweater close around her chest as if she intuits our silent presences right beside her—but I know she doesn't. She can't.

She could never imagine how quiet our quiet is—Rose's and mine—without the intake or exhalation of breath, without the thumping of a heart rhythmically squeezing and releasing, without the chemical sizzle of synapses sparking.

Death's quiet is so deep, so complete, so clear, so frigid, so pure, that it fills us until we radiate stillness the way icebergs broadcast cold.

A black Chevy Malibu appears from the east, crosses Fairfax, slows and drifts past the newspaper stand and the bus shelter, and turns to enter the driveway to the Johnie's parking lot. The windows are tinted, obscuring the driver and any passengers inside.

Does Cali recognize the car? She stays where she is, but follows it with her eyes.

Then the housekeeper I saw in Elaine's kitchen approaches Cali from the driveway. Gloria. She wears a coat over a turquoise blue nightgown and bedroom slippers. Her silver-flecked black hair is pulled back into a long, thick braid.

With her is a tall, lean young man in his twenties—this must be Roberto. Roberto wears dark jeans and a white t-shirt.

When Cali sees Gloria, she runs to meet her, then throws herself against Gloria's small, ample form and begins to cry.

"Que va a estar bien," Gloria murmurs gently and strokes Cali's hair. "Que va a estar bien."

Chapter 32

"Since we're all going to die, it's obvious that when and how don't matter."

Albert Camus

But Roberto doesn't appear to be confident that things will work out for the best. He frowns at Cali. "I think I should drive you home," Roberto says.

"Please," Cali says urgently. "Please. I can't go home! Can I go to your house, Gloria? Please?"

"If you have some kind of problem, then you belong at your own house. That is the right thing. For you. For me. And especially for my mother."

"I can't go home right now," Cali says. "Please don't make me go home. Please."

Gloria puts her arm around Cali's shoulder and says something to Roberto in Spanish. His eyes darken and he turns and walks in quick, long strides toward his car. Gloria and Cali follow him, Gloria holding Cali's hand in hers.

Roberto opens the door on the passenger side and nods to Cali who climbs in the back seat. Rose and I move with Cali and Rose arranges herself between Cali and me. Gloria gets in the front with Roberto.

Sometimes the living travel just like the dead—cocooned in an elastic and spongy silence. Roberto drives west on Wilshire then north on Crescent Heights all the way to Sunset and then over Laurel Canyon.

Cali sits staring straight ahead. Every few minutes her new cell phone buzzes in her hand, displaying text messages from Zen or Marissa—"where r u bitch?" "hey bitch, r u drowned yet?"

Roberto continues north past Ventura Boulevard, then turns west on Oxnard. After a few miles he turns again.

Squat apartment buildings sit on both sides of the street. They have names like The Calcutta, Oxnard Regal, The Oxnard Isle—there are no islands that I can see despite these exotic names, not even traffic islands—before he slows at The Valley Grotto.

Have Elaine or Steve discovered that Cali is gone?

And if they have—what are they doing about it?

Roberto turns into an impossibly narrow driveway, then into a narrow below-building parking space with the number 11 painted on the wall.

Gloria gets out of the car and nods for Cali to get out, too. Cali hops out of the back seat, slams the car door and follows Gloria and Roberto into a courtyard and up concrete stairs to a second floor apartment overlooking a tiny swimming pool.

A dog on the other side of the door starts to yap as Roberto removes some keys from his pocket and opens the security screen door and then the scuffed brown door to the apartment.

Gloria enters the apartment first, then Cali, Rose and I, and finally Roberto. A Chihuahua with a serious overbite barks and dances joyfully around Gloria's slippered feet.

Rose is fascinated with the little dog. She presses her face close to his, trying to sniff the dogs tiny face and then to nose its wildly wagging tail.

The dog turns his attention toward Cali, barking and jumping around her boots. Cali smiles and drops to her knees. She extends her hand for the dog to sniff, then scratches behind his tiny ears.

Seeing Cali with this dog reminds me that Elaine never allowed her to have a pet. Elaine's excuse was that she was allergic—to dogs and cats and—to anything she didn't like or didn't want around.

Roberto has switched on the overhead light, one square glass fixture in the pockmarked lunar surface of the beige cottage cheese ceiling. The light reveals that the living room is tiny and opens to a very small galley kitchen. Gloria has vacuumed the shit out of the beige wall-to-wall shag carpet, producing razor-straight stripes along its surface. A brown velveteen couch with a bright crocheted blanket folded on it is pressed against the wall. Jesus, nailed to the cross, his eyes turned upward in agony, is enclosed within a thin glass picture frame above the couch.

Father, why hast thou forsaken me?

A small television sits on a plastic table across from Jesus and the couch. Framed school photographs of Roberto sit on top of the TV. From the look of them, Roberto forgot how to smile after the third grade.

If Gloria has or had a husband there is no sign of him.

Cali isn't sure what to do—she sits on the floor with the dog in her lap as Roberto disappears into one of three narrow doors that open off a tiny hallway past the living room. Rose floats next to Cali's head. I hover in the middle of the room.

Awkward, awkward all around.

Gloria emerges from the kitchen holding a dog biscuit in her hand. She tosses it in the air for the Chihuahua who leaps to the carpet and catches it in his teeth. Rose's eyes are wide as he noisily consumes the bone-shaped biscuit.

"Senorita Cali," Gloria says. "Are you hungry?"

"No thank you," Cali says. "I'm fine. Gracias."

"I can make the quesadilla you like. Or hot milk and Mexican chocolate."

The sound of a toilet flushing interrupts Gloria.

"I'm fine, really, Gloria." Cali says. "And I can just sleep here right on the couch. Don't worry."

Roberto returns to the living room in time to hear Cali say this.

"One night." Roberto says looking at his mother. "Uno noche." Roberto takes a step toward Cali and lowers his face close to hers to emphasize his message, causing Rose to release a deep growl from her skinny belly.

I move to Rose and pat her forehead.

"Roberto!" Gloria says. "No."

"Uno noche," Roberto repeats. "One night and you're on your own. And you do anything, anything at all, to get my mother in trouble—you'll have to answer to me."

Chapter 33

I don't like to admit it, but sour, forgot-how-to-smile una-noche Roberto has a point. Why should Gloria do anything for Cali?

When I was alive and living with Cali, she—just like her mother—never did a thing in the house except to demand and to consume.

She never made her bed. Never smoothed a bedspread over the sheets. Never did laundry. Never picked up a towel or an article of clothing—which Gloria had washed, folded, ironed or retrieved from the dry cleaners—from the spot where she'd relinquished it to the floor that Gloria or someone like her had recently and thoroughly vacuumed, mopped and polished. Never rinsed a glass or put a dirty dish in the dishwasher. Never cooked a meal. Never carried a plate or empty Coke can down the stairs and into the kitchen. Gloria arrived early and disappeared late—long after the dinner she cooked, served and cleaned up after was over—leaving only quiet and orderliness behind for her wanton employers to destroy during the night.

Now Gloria unfolds a crisply ironed white sheet across the couch, unfurls the pink crocheted blanket, fluffs up a pillow for Cali, then sits beside Cali and strokes her hair until she drifts into a troubled sleep.

Rose has curled up next to the dog in the one object that isn't beige—a purple padded dog bed that sits next to the brown couch. But the dog is restless. He jumps up and trots to Gloria, and, to Rose's shock and delight, sits up and begs. Then he runs to the front door and scratches it, whining softly.

"Roberto," Gloria says softly to Roberto in the kitchen, "Peter needs to go out."

Rose eagerly follows Peter and Roberto out of the apartment, down the stairs, past the pool and out into the street. I follow Rose. Peter now wears a leopard print halter that connects him to Roberto with a matching leash.

Old cars and oversized trucks claim every parking space on the street. Some cars have breached the curb and occupy the narrow strips of grass in front of the apartments. Roberto patiently follows Peter along the sidewalk, allowing him to stop and sniff anything that interests his tiny nose—dog shit, vomit, a fast food burger wrapper.

Rose—unable to enjoy the smells—enjoys observing Peter. In life she was never taken for a walk. Never attended to. Never free to go beyond a short rope's radius.

After a time Peter stops and circles a small area of withering grass under a telephone pole, then lifts his tiny leg and releases a stream of urine against the pole. Rose is right behind him, entranced, as if Peter were riding a skateboard or surfing.

When Peter is finished, he kicks the grass with his back feet. Now Rose decides it's her turn. She squats in the air below the pole and tries to pee over Peter's spot, then tries to kick the grass, too. Poor Rose. She has nothing liquid left inside her gaunt form with which make her mark upon the living world.

When Roberto is a block away from the apartment, he stops and dials a number on his cell phone, then waits for what feels like long time for the person on the other end to pick up.

"Mrs. Green," he says—a statement, not a question— and then Roberto pauses as someone makes sounds on the other end.

"A friend. A family friend."

More mumbling now, which, from the look on his face, annoys Roberto.

Roberto speaks more loudly now. "Who I am doesn't matter. Go check your daughter's room and you'll see she's not where she's supposed to be."

Shit.

The tinny voice on the cell phone speaker has Elaine's nasal quality, its annoying lilt.

As Roberto listens, he looks down and sees that Peter has found a dried out chicken wing on the grass. Roberto covers the phone and grabs the bone. When Roberto tosses the bone across the street, Peter's feelings are hurt and Rose is confused.

Now I think I recognize Steve's voice if he had become an insect.

"Enough" Roberto says, "I know where your daughter is. Do you understand?"

Steve again.

"She's fine. But she needs to go home," Roberto says. "And I know that if I call the police and tell them she's not with you, she'll go to jail. Promise to keep innocent people out of this, and I'll tell you where she is."

Chapter 34

"Death is ...a gap you can't see, and when the wind blows through it, it makes no sound ..."

Tom Stoppard

Rose has again folded herself in the air above Peter's small dog bed—a novelty to a chained dog who slept on the open ground.

Her lovely eyes study Peter's tiniest movements while her sensitive ears, one higher than the other—listen to Cali breathe.

I suppose I understand why Roberto called Elaine and Steve.

But I wish he hadn't.

It would have been better if Cali had called them herself and begged their forgiveness for running off again.

I have spent the night waiting for the bad thing I know is about to happen to happen.

Whatever it is will be fueled by Elaine's vanity and Steve's anger.

But something is wrong, very wrong.

Whatever Elaine and Steve decided to do should have been done by now.

Chapter 35

"...to die is different from what any one supposed, and luckier."

Walt Whitman

Still nothing.

Roberto walked Peter and then told Gloria he was going to the gym.

Now it's almost noon.

What am I missing?

Gloria—dressed in black slacks and a crisply ironed pink blouse—throws a bone-shaped biscuit across the living room to Peter. As Peter digs it out of the thick shag carpet, Gloria urges Cali out the door and then shuts it quickly. After a backward look at Peter, Rose passes swiftly through the door. I follow Rose.

The two women walk down the stairs and then out to the front of the building where they appear to be waiting for someone. Gloria opens her large handbag—one I recognize now as what must be one of Elaine's castoffs—and removes a small purple umbrella, then opens it and uses it as a sunshade.

Did I mention Elaine's closet to you? She had it redone right before the divorce and it is twice as big as Gloria's apartment. Special closet designers came in and built display cases and installed chandeliers and tiny white spotlights that shine upon row after row of shiny high heels, boots, huge leather handbags—their hardware sparkling—and baskets overflowing with cashmere sweaters and silk scarves. It looked like a fucking boutique.

Elaine—like many of the women she knew—would replenish her closet shelves and baskets weekly, discarding seldom worn or unused clothing and accessories to make room for fresher and more expensive items.

So it was not unusual to see Gloria or the other women who worked in the house or the homes nearby wearing an employer's once-prized designer clothing as they walked to the bus stops at the end of the work day or waited for their ride back to a less exclusive zip code.

The sunlight travels through the umbrella's thin fabric and saturates Gloria's hair, skin, lips and her blouse in violet. Cali, too, absorbs the purple light, her blue irises as dark as plums.

A few cars pass by. Then a cream-colored van stops opposite Gloria and Cali. The van is nondescript except for a Jesús Me Ama bumper sticker, a red heart under Ama.

"That's the church bus," Gloria says to Cali, collapsing the umbrella. Cali looks at the van but it's hard to tell what she's thinking as she follows Gloria inside.

Most of the seats are already occupied. A woman holds the hand of a small boy on the seat next to her. An elderly couple, and a family with a daughter about Cali's age nod to Gloria and she nods in return as she chooses seats for herself and for Cali.

Rose stays very close to Cali inside the van, occupying the narrow space above Cali and Gloria.

The driver slides the van door shut and returns to the front. As he starts the motor he calls out, "Dios le bendiga!"

"Dios le bendiga!" the passengers—except Cali—echo in unison.

He drives the van west on Oxnard, then north on Sepulveda, then turns again—I'm not sure where but it seems to be zoned for auto repair—until he stops in front of the fenced-in parking lot between an auto repair yard and an LADOT yard full of yellow street maintenance vehicles.

Rose migrates through the van's back window—then poised mid-air like a dragonfly—waits for Cali and Gloria to exit the van's sliding door along with its other riders. They pass through an opening in a black iron fence that surrounds the lot and walk toward a small beige building in the back. The words Sanctuaria Pentecostal del Norte have been hand-painted in downward-sloping red block letters next to the door. Rose stays ahead of me as I follow her through the bright early afternoon sunlight—made brighter by the absence of trees—into the small building.

Once inside I see that Gloria's church is just a big room. No pews. No stained glass windows. No decoration. The bottom half of the walls are brown and the tops are white. Wall-to-wall forest green industrial carpeting muffles the entering churchgoers' footsteps. People greet one another in Spanish or stand in front of rows of those white plastic lawn chairs they sell at the drugstore. Whoever invented those shitty chairs must be a billionaire by now. They're everywhere. I'm sure there are thousands at the bottom of the ocean and soon they will litter the craters of the moon.

There is a podium at one end of the room. A few people stand near the podium with a small band. The vibe is calm but disorganized—the place feels more like an airline terminal in which people mill around than any church I've ever seen.

The band begins to play--two electric guitars and a keyboard—with the keyboard guy singing a song in Spanish that includes the words "Jesus," Dios" and "corazon."

Gloria embraces various people as she moves toward the front of the room, then leads Cali close to the podium. Gloria begins to sway slightly to the music.
Cali and Rose remain very still and watch Gloria with curiosity. The song ends and Gloria and the others clap enthusiastically and shout "Hallelujah."

The band begins another song—"A Cristo, solo a Cristo, yo Exaltare. A Cristo, solo a Cristo, Yo adorare. Porque el me ha dado vida eterna. Porque el me ha dado el poder."

Gloria sings along this time—her body rocking back and forth—her eyes closed, one open palm lifted to the air, the other palm folded around Cali's hand—"A Cristo, solo a Cristo, Yo adorare." Others sing and move in the same way and I see that singing this song is a powerful form of prayer, not so different from the davening I've seen in synagogues.

Cali remains straight and still, her eyes on Gloria, her hand in Gloria's.

A heavy man in a white shirt and khaki pants approaches the podium and joins in singing the song's final chorus—"Porque el me ha dado el poder."

Because He has given me the power. What power is that, I wonder. What power could Gloria possibly have around Elaine and all the women like her?

There are more loud hallelujahs as the song dies and the band begins another—Santo, santo santo dicen los serafines. Santo, santo santo es el señor Jehova. Santo, santo, santo al dios que nos redime, por ser tres veces santo, la tierra llena de su gloria esta, el cielo y la tierra pasaran, mas su palabra no pasara.

The man at the podium sings into the microphone, both his hands lifted heavenward, tears flowing now from his closed eyes. The faithful begin weep, to cry out, to move their bodies more urgently to the rhythm of the song.

What does Cali think? What does Rose feel? Theirs are the only still and quiet places in the room of swaying, rocking, murmuring, shouting and sobbing faithful.

"Santo, santo, santo!" This time the loud, ecstatic voice declaring holiness is Gloria's.

She releases Cali's hand and raises her arms above her head, then begins to spin. The purse that was once Elaine's falls to the floor and Cali picks it up. Two men near the front row of chairs rush to Gloria, but do not touch her as her body is overcome with shaking.

"Los espíritus están con nosotros! Los espíritus se ve!" Gloria proclaims.

Spirits are among us. Spirits are here.

Gloria's trembling becomes convulsive and the whites of her eyes are visible as she spins around, then leans toward the empty space I occupy behind Rose.

"Un pero espiritu!" Gloria bends forward and passes her hands through Rose.

"Un hombre muerto gordo!" I have no idea what "gordo" means, but "dead man" I understand.

Gloria swivels toward me and lunges—her head moving through me like a knife in water.

Holy shit.

Does Gloria see us?

Pero and muerto.

Does Gloria really know we're here?

Cali holds the purse tightly to her chest.

Then Gloria lurches backwards and the men break her fall onto the soft green carpet where she shakes some more. Gloria's eyelids flip open like a doll's. "Para usted! Para usted, señorita Cali! Usted está en peligro."

For you. For you, Miss Cali. The spirit dog and the gordo dead man are for you. You are in danger.

Chapter 36

"...let us deprive death of its strangeness, let us frequent it, let us get used to it..."

Montaigne

Gloria's eyelids close. She convulses on the green carpet, the podium man holding her hand, a kneeling woman stroking her forehead.

"What is wrong with her?" Cali asks, shock on her pale face.

The podium man looks at Cali and smiles.

"Don't worry, Senorita," he says. "It is el mano de Dios! Look! The hand of God touches your friend! "lla es con el Espíritu Santo. She is among the spirits now."

Gloria's back arches, her head shakes from side to side, and her pink tongue is visible as the unintelligible voice of God spills from her mouth.

Chapter 37

"...death is the key which unlocks the door to our true happiness."

Wolfgang Amadeus Mozart

Does Gloria remember her vision?

Does she remember what she said?

And whether she does or not—what does it mean?

Until now I was certain—absolutely certain—that only the dead could visit the dead.

That only the dead could see the dead.

Now I'm not so sure.

What was really happening to Gloria?

Was she hallucinating?

What did she really see?

Whatever it was—Gloria was as fully warm and alive as Cali is.

And—as Gloria boards the van with Cali after the church service ends—she is as demure and untroubled as she was before.

Now if I were living and in a moment of religious ecstasy the veil separating the living from the dead was lifted——I'd be a little fucking agitated.

And maybe scared shitless, too.

But Gloria is tranquil—like the glassy surface of a deep lake when the wind has stopped.

On the van ride home Gloira watches the not very lovely world of so-called gentlemen's clubs and muffler shops pass by her window as if she were looking at the Champs Elysees. And once inside her apartment she unremarkably turns on the small television and listens to a telenovela while preparing a lunch of tuna salad sandwiches for herself and for Cali.

How's that for an anticlimax?

Peter trots close to the table and his tiny nostrils flare as he inhales the tuna's rich and complex scent, a mixture of seawater, fish flesh and death. Rose follows him, unable to smell the food, but still fascinated by everything he does.

Gloria brings two glasses of water to the table, sits down and smoothes a paper napkin on her lap. This is Peter's cue to dance on his hind legs and to yap.

"Oh, Peter," Gloria says, "Tienes hambre? Here is your tuna sandwich, Peter."
Gloria gives Peter one of the triangles and he carries it between his teeth to his dog bed where he consumes it with one bite. Rose follows him and watches, satisfied just to see Peter loved and fed.

Now it is Gloria's turn, and she takes small bites from her sandwich, her face turned toward the television.

I'm waiting.

Jesus in his agony on the wall is waiting—too—for Gloria to acknowledge what happened at church.

But Gloria watches the TV and does not speak.

Cali eats the corner of one sandwich. "This is great, Gloria. Thank you."

Gloria nods. "Gracias, Senorita Cali."

"And thank you so much for having me. I just can't go home right now. I hope you understand."

Then Gloria turns away from the television screen. "At church I prayed for you, Senorita Cali." Gloria looks serious now. "Jesus will help you, Senorita Cali. I know He will. He sent you the angels to save you."

Rose I get—but in what fucking universe could an angel possibly be me?

Gloria remembers her vision all right, but it's obviously distorted—like an image in a carnival mirror that seems very vague and very far away.

Cali nods confusedly. "So it's okay if I stay here for a little while longer? I really can't go home right now. It's complicated, but believe me when I tell you that I haven't done anything wrong."

Gloria puts her sandwich on the plate, then turns and embraces Cali. "Even when we are in danger, Jesus knows what to do." Gloria glances at the picture on the wall behind her.

Jesus remains noncommittal. Silent.

The only sound that competes with the television comes from outside. Footsteps are audible on the stairs, then the murmur of male voices and an insistent knocking on the door.

Peter growls, then runs to the door, letting out high-pitched yips that hurt even my dead ears.

"Mrs. Garcia?" A male voice enquires from the other side of the door. "Mrs. Garcia? I'm Officer Zachary from the Van Nuys police station. I'd like to have a word with you."

Peter alternates high-pitched barks with loud snuffling sounds, then presses his nose to the bottom of the front door and tries to smell the source of the noise outside, then to dig his way outside through the carpet.

The napkin falls from her lap to the carpet as a confused Gloria rises from the couch and turns, but Cali's hand on her arm stops her progress toward the door. Cali shakes her head no, then presses her finger to her lips to warn Gloria to remain quiet and to stay away from the door.

"Mrs. Garcia? We know you're there. Some neighbors saw you and a young woman enter your apartment. Please open the door. It's very important that we speak to you."

A different male voice speaks now. "Senora Garcia. Abra la puerta, por favor. "

"God is watching over you," Gloria whispers and walks to the door. "God and the angels." Cali seems frozen on the couch.

Rose turns away from Peter and sails across the room to be near her.

Gloria picks up Peter and then holds him tightly as she opens the door. A tall young uniformed police officer enters first, and then a shorter man who appears a little older.

"Mrs. Garcia?" The tall officer asks Gloria. Peter squirms and snaps at the officer. Rose floats in front of Cali as if to shield her.

Gloria takes a few steps back. "Ssshh, Peter," she says.

The tall cop enters the apartment. The short officer ducks into the kitchen then goes into the bathroom and the two bedrooms, as if he's looking for someone. Peter hates this and resumes barking.

"What is your name, Miss?" The tall cop looks at Cali.

Cali takes a long time to answer the question. "My name is Cali Green."

Chapter 38

*"What will you ever do before Death's knife
Provides the answer ultimate and appropriate?"*

Delmore Schwartz

Peter's hysterical yapping disturbs the sombre quiet as the police officers escort Cali and Gloria down the stairs. Gloria has left him, his bed, his bowl, his biscuits and some cans of dog food with a neighbor. An assortment of passers-by make room for the two uniformed policemen as they escort Gloria and Cali—and without their knowing it, Rose and me—into their black and white police car parked in a red zone in front of a fire hydrant.

Cali's face glistens with tears. Gloria, frightened and confused, glances back worriedly toward the upstairs apartment that is the source of Peter's baleful and insistent barking, as the officers get into the front seat and drive off quickly.

The only sounds are garbled bursts from the police radio during the short drive to the LAPD Van Nuys Division building near the courthouse government center complex.

I remind myself that neither Cali nor Gloria is under arrest. All the officers would say, first in English and then in Spanish, is that Gloria and Cali are urgently needed at the station.

The black-and-white moves past bail bonds offices and the bright red Happy Dogs hot dog stand on Van Nuys Boulevard, and then turns onto Sylmar Street and into a parking structure.

Officer Zachary opens the door and nods toward Gloria. She gets out of the car and Cali slides out after her. Rose is behind Cali, but close to me. Rose doesn't like the uniforms. And she hates cages. That wire screen dividing the back from the front in the police car distresses her. The other policeman walks ahead and holds the glass door open for Gloria, who enters the lobby with her head bowed as if she's getting ready for an execution.

Zachary leads the women into a hallway off the lobby and behind the reception area, then opens a door on which is a sign that says, "Meeting Room One." "Miss Stone, we appreciate your cooperation today. Your family is eager to see you."

Defeat clouds Cali's expression as Officer Zachary opens the door to reveal Elaine, Steve, Mr. Christian and a bald policeman in plain clothes seated around a table.

"Oh my God!" Elaine cries and rushes toward Cali. "My baby is safe! She's safe from that monster!"

Jesus. You'd think Elaine was raving about Grendel's mother, not the small, frightened woman, one arm clutching her purse, who gently leads Cali into the room.

"I want to stay with her." Cali says, turning away from Elaine and standing close to Gloria.

"I'm sorry, Miss. But you'll have to wait in here. With your family." Officer Zachary repeats, this time as a command. "Mrs. Garcia will have to be questioned in a separate room."

Still Cali resists. "I go where she goes."

Christian, the lawyer, appears in the hallway and smiles at the two police officers. "It's understandable that you're confused, Cali," he says smoothly. "After what you've been through and your recent treatment for emotional instability. But your parents are waiting for you."

Cali throws her arms around Gloria, but the policeman who speaks Spanish tugs Gloria away, and a heavy policewoman, who has appeared suddenly from around the corner, places her hand firmly on Gloria's arm.

"It's okay, Senorita Cali," Gloria says. "Go to your mother now." Cali stands outside the room and watches as Gloria is led a little way down the hall and disappears into a room.

Cali enters the room, sobbing. Rose follows her and curls up above the scuffed and empty table, her head on her paws, her sad eyes registering Cali's misery. Elaine sits again at the table close to Cali and to Steve. Christian sits near the bald policeman in street clothes.

The room has one rectangular window that opens not to the outdoors, but to the next room. At first the rectangle is dark but then the light goes on, illuminating the small space in which Gloria sits alone, her arms clutching Elaine's old purse on her lap.

The window is a two-way mirror.

Elaine—dressed in high boots, a long gray cashmere sweater and tight cashmere pants—begins to yell when she sees Gloria.

"That monster took my child!" Elaine shouts. "Just look at her."

Cali backs away from Elaine and the officer, stopping when she has reached the corner of the room. Rose barks, then sails in front of Cali, trying to protect her. But Elaine won't be stopped. She totters on her high boots toward Cali, her large and boxy leather handbag—full of gleaming latches and zippers—passes through Rose, and pushes herself against Cali in an awkward approximation of an embrace.

Cali shouts at Elaine. "Leave me alone!"

The bald policeman's eyes widen and Steve and Christian exchange a look.

Steve walks to Elaine and puts his arms around her shoulders, then arranges his features into a sad and philosophical expression. Steve speaks loudly. "It's okay, Cali. Gloria can't hurt you now."

"What are you talking about?" Cali asks.

The bald policeman finally speaks. "Don't worry, Miss Green. Although you can see and hear her, Mrs. Garcia can't hear you. We know that Gloria Garcia was holding you against your will."

"What?" Cali asks again. "I asked Gloria if I could stay with her. It was my idea."

Christian smiles knowingly. "This is very common, isn't that right Captain Brown? Kidnap victims often identify with their captors and blame themselves for their abduction."

"All Gloria did was be nice to me. Do you hear me? Gloria did nothing wrong!"

"Calm down, Cali," Christian says now. He stands and looks toward the bald policeman, Elaine and Steve. "We all understand exactly what you're feeling and we understand that you're confused."

Captain Brown nods and leaves the room. A moment later he reappears on the other side of the mirror with the heavyset uniformed policewoman. They both stand close to Gloria.

Cali stands still and watches. Elaine and Steve are frozen, too. Christian smiles his tight-ass, lawyerly smile.

The bald officer nods to Gloria, then his voice becomes audible through a speaker in the wall. "Mrs. Garcia, when Miss Green is more composed, it is very likely that you will face kidnapping charges. But right now you are under arrest for grand theft."

Gloria looks dazed as the female cop Mirandizes her, takes her hands and deftly snaps metal handcuffs around her trembling wrists.

"Theft? You know Gloria doesn't steal! " Cali shouts at Elaine, then presses her face against the two-way mirror.

On the other side of the glass, the bald officer picks up Gloria's purse from the table and, holding the strap between his fingers as if it's radioactive, follows Gloria and the female officer out the door.

"Gloria stole my purse," Elaine says smugly. "Do you think she can afford a designer handbag on her salary?"

"What?" Cali says, confused.

The unctuous Christian is more than happy to explain: "See your mother's three thousand dollar Givenchy handbag being taken into evidence?" Christian points to the two way mirror.

"Your amigo Gloria is a thief."

Chapter 39

"...the opposite of life is not death, it's indifference."

Elie Wiesel

Elaine's bloated Beverly Hills mega-fucking-residence seems even more enormous. I'm sure the cars that drive past its gated entrance, the sparrows and scrub jays whose wings slice the dark sky above it, and the L.A. Times delivery guy feel small, incredibly small.

But isn't making people feel small the point of a house like this?

I know I am made less—of whatever I have become— just by being near it—not to mention the recent events which have made me feel that I am disintegrating like a rice paper flower in a cup of warm water.

I already had a bad case of post-mortal humilitas. Jesus. A pet rock has more mojo than I do dead.

Why did Elaine and Steve insist on charging Gloria with unlawful possession of an out-of-fashion designer pocketbook that Elaine gave Gloria years ago?

Because they could.

And because hurting Gloria would be a useful demonstration of what happens when you cross them—were you watching, Cali Green?

Before coming here, I took Rose to visit Peter at the apartment. He was subdued as Roberto spoke on the phone to a legal aid place about helping his mother get out of jail.

Now—before passing through the walls of Elaine's Everest of an abode—I urge her to enjoy the velvety grass outside.

But Rose quickly melts through the thick front doors, then flows through the foyer and up the grand staircase, not stopping until she is a few inches from Cali, asleep in a tangle of Elaine's 1200 thread count bed sheets.

Did I mention the man?

Rose passed through him, too—a muscular guy in navy blue scrubs who sits right now just outside Cali's bedroom door. On a small table near him are a pitcher of water and three plastic bottles of pills—Ativan. Ambien. Haldol.

Chapter 40

"It is hard to have patience with people who say 'There is no death' or 'Death doesn't matter.' ... You might as well say that birth doesn't matter."

C.S. Lewis

What time is it? One or two A.M.? Rose hovers above Cali's sheet-draped form while I—transparent as a jellyfish—drift inside the quiet darkness of Cali's room.

Then the low hum of voices reaches us. I move to Rose, wishing I could stroke her forehead and feel the bones of her skull under my gray fingers. "I'm going downstairs. I'm not sure for how long. Stay. Stay with Cali."

How can a dog that lived chained to a pole understand the request to "stay"? Does Rose understand that I don't feel right leaving Cali alone? That I need to find out what is going on?

But Rose descends closer to the surface of the bed as if my words exert a downward force.

Of course. Her sensitive ears picked up the voices long before mine did.

I pass through Cali's bedroom door, then right through the guy in scrubs sitting outside the door. He wears one earbud in his left ear and I see that he is watching porn on a small tablet.

I descend to the first floor, then locate the source of the voice in the room Elaine calls "the library." A strip of light glows beneath the closed, thick carved wood "library" door. I ooze right through.

Dark wood bookshelves extend from the polished floor to the high arched ceilings. Recessed spotlights illuminate the rows of books, age and wear distressing their erect leather and gilt spines. But if you look closely at the artfully worn sets of Dickens, Shakespeare, Rousseau, Wordsworth, Montaigne, Faulkner, Thoreau, Flaubert, Locke, Chaucer, Spenser, Donne, Poe, and the others—which no one except Gloria does when she dusts each week—you can see they're fakes, some of the volumes glued together to serve as false fronts to cupboards hiding a wide screen TV and Steve's video games.

But the leaded glass windows and heavy wine-colored drapes, the large brass chandelier, the English tsotchkes—the ugly Chinoiserie dogs, Toby mugs, and marble busts of thoughtful old men—cannot persuade the living people gathered here in the middle of the night they are in London and are not—alas—still in Beverly Fucking Hills.

Elaine, Steve, and Christian—dressed in casual street clothes as if they are all about to go out for a walk—and three people I do not know—two muscular, tan men in their late twenties wearing khaki pants and navy blue hoodies, and a woman in her thirties, same hoodie but wearing gray slacks—sit close together in the coffee-colored leather chairs that are supposed to make you feel you're inside an exclusive London men's club. Except that the illusion is spoiled by the enormous, ludicrous and forever-glistening oil portrait of Elaine and Steve that hangs above the fireplace in a fake baroque frame with its own faux baroque lighting fixture.

Elaine—a Madame Tussaud's wax figure in a royal blue evening gown rendered by the painter as a furious froth of crude brushstrokes—looks down haughtily from inside the ornate frame. Next to her stands Steve—taller than he really is—his visage rendered an orangey tan that the painter thought would indicate good health. Instead of his preppy gear, portrait Steve sports a red tie and navy blue blazer with large gold buttons, a thick blob of white paint on each button to signifying their shiny and expensive brassiness.

Painted Steve's eyes' focus is on something far away—probably his and Elaine's glorious future—. But in life Steve, in jeans and his Buddhism Center t-shirt, keeps his eyes down and stares at a small duffel bag and a pile of clothing on the oriental carpeted floor—a pair of Cali's very skinny jeans, a pair of tennis shoes, a pair of socks, a bra and underpants and a black hooded sweatshirt.

What now? Why in the middle of the night?

The woman speaks. She has short, curly ginger-red hair, sun-reddened cheeks and deep blue eyes--like a Hummel figurine come to life. Her bare, strawberry blond eyelashes give her a wholesome, healthy look as if she makes her living on a dairy farm or tapping trees for maple syrup. She has a sheaf of printed forms on her lap and holds a couple ballpoint pens in her hand. "I know you're worried, Mr. and Mrs. Cansler," she says kindly, "but rest assured that you are doing the very best thing you can possibly do to help your daughter."

Christian breaks in. "And, Elaine, we're doing the only thing that will satisfy the court at this juncture, and that will address Cali's legal," he pauses—"entanglements."

Elaine nods. Steve lifts his head and meets Christian's gaze, but says nothing. I can see the ropey muscles inside Steve's cheeks and neck working. Whatever is going on, there is real tension in this room.

The woman smiles and takes one of Elaine's manicured hands and squeezes it with her unadorned one. "Mrs. Cansler, I understand what you and your child are going through. And know that I've seen with my own eyes that the state of the art therapeutic wilderness curriculum that Serene Mountain offers has saved many students with problems much, much worse than your daughter's."

"State of the art" is nice. Elaine's eyes glisten.

The woman keeps going. "The school is transformational—that's the only way I can describe it. You'll see."

She's good. How many times has she delivered this pitch?

Elaine seems not to notice the slickness of the delivery and smiles, "I'm sure you're right, Ms. Morris."

"Rita," the woman says.

"Rita," Elaine repeats. "But Cali is such a city girl, I'm not sure how she'll adjust to all the outdoor activity."

Rita smiles as if the slot machine she's been working all night has just delivered the jackpot she was sure would come. "Of course you worry. You're a mom, right?"

I hate the word, "mom." I fucking hate it.

"But a city girl is the right candidate for what we offer. At Serene Mountain we've discovered that the less familiar the experience, the more effective it is for our students. A clean break from unhealthy patterns and unwholesome influences is exactly what your daughter needs. Now, if you'll just sign these forms."

Rita passes some of the printed forms to Elaine, the rest to Steve, and resumes talking, her voice soothing and maple syrupy. "This one, Mrs. and Mr. Cansler, just says that you place your daughter under the care and supervision of Serene Mountain. And this one is a health history form--you know, allergies, immunization record, and stuff like that. The last one is just an emergency contact form—names, dates, addresses, contact numbers."

Elaine glances at the forms while Rita's voice lowers to a purr. "The sooner your daughter is transported to Serene Mountain, the sooner we can help her turn her life around." Rita turns toward the two men and smiles again, "Transport is what Witt and Kirby will be helping Cali with in a just few minutes. They are an expert extraction team."

The two men nod.

Transport? Extraction team? Whatever boarding school Cali is going to, why don't Elaine and Steve drive her there themselves? Or have that creep Christian do it? I'm sure he'd be happy to—for a price.

"Kirby and Witt have handled some very difficult extractions with real professionalism. And they have ten years of transport experience between them," Rita adds, as if that is a very good thing, and as if what they will be "transporting" is something volatile, toxic and dangerous— like a lethal and highly infectious virus—not a teenaged girl.

As Elaine fills in, initials, and signs the forms, Rita says, "I trust that Mr. Christian has gone over the extraction and transport scenario with you? I am happy to answer any questions."

Steve finally speaks. "Mrs. Cansler and I are fine with the program. And the transport."

Even Steve can't bring himself to say "extraction."

"But can you go over the fees again? Since this is already late October, and taking into account Thanksgiving and holiday vacations, it seems only fair that the first semester tuition be pro-rated."

Fees. Fucking fees.

"Of course," Rita says, as if she's eager for the opportunity to talk numbers with Steve. "Let me start with the fees: Transport is billed separately from tuition. Transport from Los Angeles to Roca Azul, including rental vehicles, hotels, food and incidentals, is $7,500 dollars without gratuity."

Witt and Kirby grin.

Roca Azul? Where are they sending her, Mexico?

"And there will be a one-time intake and processing fee of $2500 that you will be billed shortly after your daughter arrives on campus. This fee will cover a comprehensive health exam including lab fees for blood and urine testing as well as in-depth psychosocial and educational assessments. We want to make sure Cali is ready for the outdoor activities and we want to know her as best we can so we can tailor our treatment to her unique needs. If you would like a more comprehensive psychiatric assessment and admissions report, I can arrange for that for an additional fee."

Christian says, "I think the additional psychiatric assessment and report would prove very useful, Steve."

Steve nods, but he doesn't look happy.

"Your daughter's monthly tuition—which will cover textbooks, course materials, state of the art wilderness gear—"

There it is again—"state of the art."

"—and room and board is $7, 800 per month. As for the vacations you mentioned, we've found that students request that they remain at Serene Mountain during their residencies and so we host Thanksgiving and other holiday celebrations for them on site. You can't imagine how beautiful it is to celebrate Thanksgiving, Christmas, Hanukkah and Kwanzaa under starlight in the snow."

Snow? It can't be Mexico.

"We'd appreciate it if you could pay Kirby and Witt the transport fee now as well as giving me the first nine months' tuition."

Nine months? What about summer vacation?

Steve glares at Christian, who returns his look with a small, grim nod.

Steve reaches into the pocket of his jeans and produces a leather checkbook with a slim silver stashed pen inside. He opens it, removes the pen, and with a flourish begins to write.

Chapter 41

"There is but one freedom, to put oneself right with death."

Albert Camus

Steve tears one check from the checkbook and hands it to Rita. After another flourish and the sound of ripping paper, he turns to either Witt or Kirby—which is which?—and gives the check to him.

"You'll see that the gratuity is included," Steve says.

Witt or Kirby accepts the check, scans, folds, then slides it into his pocket.

"Much appreciated," Witt or Kirby says.

Rita sighs as if she has just witnessed Venus's miraculous birth from the clam shell and something even more wonderful is about to happen next—perhaps benevolent and not so horrible-looking aliens from a more advanced civilization are landing right now on the sweeping front lawn. "Awesome!" she exclaims.

God, I hate that word.

"There's one more thing I'm going to give you—I'm sorry to burden you with so much paper—but this explains more about our intake process and what Cali will be experiencing in the next few months."

Months. At least nine months she said.

Rita holds up a glossy color brochure. On the cover is a photograph of a teenaged girl and boy at the summit of a squarish rocky mountain. The sky above the mountain is sea blue. Decorative white clouds that might be Photoshopped adorn the sky. The kids—in plaid flannel shirts and carrying backpacks—appear triumphantly happy. Above their faces is printed, "Serene Mountain Retreat: Treatment. Education. Strength. Renewal. For Troubled Teens."

"'Most of our students lose weight. But they also gain muscle.'" Elaine reads from the brochure. "'...thanks to increased physical activity and a wholesome diet free of junk food.'" Elaine smiles. "Well, that sounds great. Maybe Steve and I should come along with Cali," she jokes.

Rita laughs. "You're not the first parent who wished that, Mrs. Cansler. But right now our program can only accept teenagers."

Christian looks at his watch and clears his throat. "It's after three," he says.

"You're right, Mr. Christian," Rita says and stands. "Now I can't stress enough that Kirby and Witt are experienced professionals. No matter how oppositional your daughter becomes during the extraction, no matter how much resistance she displays, please do not give in to the urge to react, to interfere or to intervene. Really, the best thing for Cali would be for you two to leave the house or to at least stay completely out of view."

"Rita's absolutely right," Christian says before Elaine or Steve can speak. "I've been through this with other clients and there's much less drama when the parents aren't around."

Elaine's slim, perfectly shaped brows briefly angle upward with doubt, but then relax. "What do you say we go to Starbucks?" she says to Steve.

Elaine and Steve stand and quickly leave the library, but not before Rita gives Elaine a quick hug. Witt, Kirby, Christian and Rita listen to the sound of their footsteps in the large foyer, then to the sound of the massive front doors opening and closing.

Christian looks at Rita as he sits down again in the leather chair. "I'll be in here if you need me. And if you don't mind, please close the door on your way out."

Elaine puts the signed forms into the duffel and hands it to Witt or Kirby. She lifts the small pile of Cali's clothing from the floor and carries it to the library door. Kirby or Witt follows her out, making sure to shut the door behind them.

Chapter 42

"Death is caused by swallowing small amounts of saliva over a long period of time."

George Carlin

I shadow Kirby, Witt and Rita up the wide, curving staircase. The sounds their footsteps make sink into the thickly padded oriental carpet and die there. The guy in scrubs quickly pockets his tablet and stands to greet them as they reach the roomy second floor landing.

"She's quiet. Probably the sedatives," the guy says.

A fucking genius.

"You'd be surprised how fast those sedatives can wear off," Kirby or Witt observes. He puts the duffel down on the floor, unzips it, moves the forms Elaine and Steve signed, and pulls out two black leather utility belts—the kind policemen wear—from which dangle heavy night sticks and steel handcuffs. There are also slots containing what look like small canisters—pepper spray?—and something that might be a Taser.

Jesus. What the hell did Christian tell these people about the slight young girl asleep in the room just on the other side of that door? They seem prepared to subdue someone big, strong and violent.

Kirby and Witt fasten the equipment belts around their waists. One of them nods to Rita. The guy in scrubs steps back and Rita moves close to Cali's bedroom door, presses her ear against it for a few seconds, the opens it quickly and steps inside. Kirby and Witt are right behind her, the small bundle of Cali's clothing still in Rita's arms.

Me? I shiver through all of them and instantly reach Cali and Rose—her tail swishing in greeting above Cali's inert shape beneath the bedclothes.

Rita switches on the sconce lamp above Cali's bed and bends down. "Cali," she says loudly, "Wake up. It's time to go."

The fur on Rose's neck rises. Cali groans and her eyelids flutter, but she does not waken.

But when Rita shakes Cali's shoulders, Rose jumps and releases an almost inaudible growl from her taut chest.

"Wake up," Rita says, louder now.

Cali's eyes open. Confused, she stares first at Rita, then at Kirby and Witt, who stand—each on one side of her bed.

"Get up." Rita orders.

Rose growls again and wedges her invisible self between Rita and Cali.

Cali's eyes register surprise and then fear as Rita grabs her shoulders and roughly lifts her upright in the bed.

"Mom!" Cali screams. "Steve! There are people in my room!"

Can Christian hear the terror in Cali's voice?

Rita, her hands still on Cali's shoulders, says, "Be quiet. Do you understand me? Shut your mouth. If you refuse to cooperate, these transport agents will be more than happy to shut it for you."

The silence within the house expands like a wet sponge.

"Who are you?" Cali pleads. "What do you want? I lost my purse so I don't have any money or credit cards. But I'm sure I can get you some."

"I told you to shut your mouth," Rita says, then slaps Cali hard across her face with an open, freckled hand.

Cali gasps, red blooming in her cheeks from the stinging blow.

Rose paws the air, growls, bares her teeth, and nips uselessly at Rita.

"You will shut up and do what you're told," Rita instructs. "Get out of bed."

Cali pushes back the sheets and swings her legs around. I can see her feet, her thighs, her whole body is trembling. Witt or Kirby move so that they flank Cali, one between her and Rita, the other behind her, between Cali and the bedroom door.

"Take off your clothes," Rita orders.

"What? Now? In front of them?" Cali protests.

"Take off your clothes," Rita repeats.

Cali looks at the door and lets out an earsplitting scream, "Mom! Mom! Help me! "Steve!"

Christian, even if he's behind the thick library's closed door, must hear Cali now.

Rose flinches at the noise and lets out a series of frantic, sharp, high-pitched barks.

Witt or Kirby covers Cali's mouth with a large hand, silencing her next scream. The other man bends Cali's arms behind her back and holds them there, but Cali fights to release herself from the two men restraining her.

Kirby and Witt easily push Cali to the floor. Rita sweeps the pile of clothing and shoes off the bed onto the floor.

One of the men holds Cali's arms while the other removes duct tape from his belt, tears off a piece and then pushes it hard against Cali's mouth.

"Get undressed and put on these clothes, or your friends here will be more than happy to do it for you." Rita says.

Rose whimpers as Witt or Kirby releases Cali's arms. Cali lies on the floor, her chest heaving, her body shaking, her eyes huge above her flaring nostrils and taped mouth.

"Now." Rita says.

Cali's eyes shine with tears as she removes her t shirt, then rolls over and pulls down the underpants she is wearing. Rita again kicks the pile of clothing.

Cali crouches to conceal her nakedness, then grabs the pair of cotton underpants, the white bra, the jeans and the sweatshirt and puts them on quickly, her thin, pale back turned back to Rita and the two men.

"Shoes." Rita nods at the shoes and Cali puts on the pair of white socks and Converse sneakers.

"Stand up." Rita orders.

Cali stands, but she's unsteady. Her eyes move to the bathroom door.

She says something but the duct tape muddles it. I think she's saying "Please."

Rita looks at Cali. Cali repeats the unintelligible word, then points to her crotch and then to the bathroom.

"Keep the door open." Rita says and nods to Witt and Kirby who stand back a step.

Cali turns slowly, takes a deliberate step or two, then sprints into the bathroom. Rita moves after her, but she's not fast enough.

Before Rita can prevent the bathroom door from closing, Cali has slammed it shut and locked it.

Chapter 43

"We trouble our life by thoughts about death, and our death by thoughts about life."

Michel de Montaigne

Rose and I melt through the bathroom door as Cali, standing on the closed toilet seat, yanks the tape from her mouth and struggles to push open the screen in the narrow window above the toilet.

If Cali gets the screen out, what will keep her keep from tumbling from the angled second story roof down to the tiled patio below?

If Cali fails, then what will these people do to her?

Cali pushes hard at the screen, grunting with exertion. But Cali cannot free it from the heavy metal frame.

I expect Witt and Kirby to break down the bathroom door at any moment, but it's hushed on the other side of the door.

Rose pivots in the air, her ears cocked. Now I hear it—a tiny rustling and a series of small metallic clicks.

The bathroom door swings opens so slowly that I feel as though I'm in a dream, but finally I can see Witt or Kirby removing a small metal tool from the lock on the bedroom side of the door and then sliding it into the pocket of his khakis.

Cali is punching the screen now, her hands lacerated, her fingernails jagged.

Rita nods at Witt or Kirby and he saunters to Cali, places his large hands around her waist, and—despite her squirms, and scream and kicks—easily lifts her off the toilet seat.

"Put me down!" Cali screams. "Mom! Steve! They're hurting me!"

Silence.

Witt or Kirby keeps Cali's feet from touching the floor as he carries her from the bathroom into the bedroom, then roughly pushes her face-first down on the floor. His partner kneels, then presses his knee sharply into Cali's lower back which causes an involuntary aah as the air is forced out of her chest. He bends Cali's arms behind her back and, quickly removing the pair of handcuffs from his belt, secures her wrists.

Rose whimpers as if she has been injured and stations herself above to Cali's head.

"One more sound and you will be Tasered," Rita warns. As if this point needed emphasis, Witt or Kirby pulls the Taser from his belt and dangles it in front of Cali's face, then tears another piece of duct tape and presses it across Cali's mouth.

Rita sighs and looks at her watch. "Get her into the car. LA traffic can be really bad, even at this hour."

Chapter 44

"In the long run we are all dead."

John Maynard Keynes

The 405 is clear. The silver Lincoln MKT Town Car slices the heavy fog into swirling gray ribbons as it speeds north. Witt and Kirby sit in the back on either side of Cali—her mouth still taped and her body secured with a seat belt—their muscled forearms resting on their thick khakied thighs.

Elaine and Steve must be on their third Starbuck's nonfat grande soy sugar-free lattes by now—the shitful cowards.

Rose has braided herself into a circle above Cali's feet, her unhappy wide eyes staring at me where I hover above her like a genie above a broken lamp.

Rita is an aggressive but careful driver. I suppose it wouldn't do to interest a police officer in the progress of this particular vehicle or in the identity of its handcuffed and muzzled occupant.

Kirby, Witt and Rita must have removed children from their homes in the dead of night many times before. Despite her efforts to resist and her escape attempt, Cali's forced exit from the house was quick, quiet and precise. The soles of Cali's black Converse sneakers never touched the floor as Kirby and Witt carried her down the stairs and through the foyer, Rita following with the small duffel bag.

There was no goodbye. No clichéd and sonorous explanation of what had just happened to Cali, or what was about to happen delivered by the always confident and always self-important Christian.

There was no Christian.

As Rose and I followed Witt, Kirby, Cali and Rita through the foyer outside, I noticed that the light under the library door had been extinguished.

Still, something in my peripheral vision made me glance back at the upstairs guest room window.

That's when I saw Christian speaking into his cell phone and watching as Kirby and Witt roughly push Cali into the back seat of the car.

Fuck you, Christian. Fuck you.

Chapter 45

Tinted windows obscure almost everything outside, so I study the car's occupants.

Cali is scared shitless and in pain. Her arms have been pinned behind her back and her mouth taped shut for hours now. Sometimes she closes her eyes, but when she does it isn't to sleep. Perhaps she's imagining ways she might escape.

Witt and Kirby each wear a single earbud. One is attached to a tablet on which an Arnold Schwarzenegger movie is playing, the other to an iPod from which I hear the repetitive rhythm of heavy metal. I suppose they each must keep an ear free to hear Rita or Cali—as if she were able to cause a disturbance.

Rita activates the GPS system on the navigation screen and glances at the map. The car is a small blue dot moving out of the city and into desert. The road the dot traverses is bright green—no traffic snarls or accidents ahead.

Just as I wonder when they will feel the need to stop—to eat—to drink coffee—to use a restroom or to stretch their legs—Rita opens the hatch of a built-in cooler between the front seats and takes out three apples and three bottles of water. "Here, Witt," she says. The guy on Cali's left, the one behind the driver's seat, reaches for them.

"Thanks," Witt says.

Cali's eyes open at the sound of Rita's voice. Rose stiffens.

At least now I can tell these two assholes apart—Witt is tall and thick. His eyes are sometimes green and sometimes gray. Kirby's eyes are a dark, unchanging brown.

As Witt reaches over Cali to give the apple and the water bottle to Kirby, Rita watches Cali's eyes from the rear view mirror, measuring Cali's reaction to not being offered any water or food.

Rita smiles—a small, tight smile for Cali's benefit—then presses another button on the navigation screen to shut off the map—Rita doesn't want Cali to know where she is.

The date and time appear on the screen and I notice the date—October 22nd—the inauspicious, retrograde and melancholy thirty-ninth anniversary of my birth.

My goddamn birth—or "Kiddie Cowboy Kid's Bow" as Daily Variety described the arrival of a second son to a "homemaker" and Happy Andy, cowboy rodeo clown and children's television star. I wonder where that high-contrast black and white publicity photo is now? Did my shit brother Mark throw it out after my murder?

If he could make a buck on it, he didn't.

Being born and dying are beyond the reach of memory. But over time, that picture became the way I understood the beginning of my life. No matter that it is impossible to recall how it felt to have sunlight warm my face or flash into my eyes for the first time—I retain a phantom recollection of exactly how hot and bright it was.

As I grew, I more and more fully became the bewildered and miserable creature in the picture—the punch line of one of my father's jokes. In the photograph, my mother, her hair short in what was the popular pixie style, squints into the very bright October sun outside the hospital in Santa Monica where I was born. My grinning father, wearing a suit, a wide cowboy-themed tie and smoking a cigarette, pushes the wheelchair in which my mother sits toward a waiting taxi cab. My older brother Mark stands to one side, lanky, slender and unsmiling.

And me? I'm bundled in an over-exposed white blanket in my mother's smooth arms, a tuft of dark hair escaping the little cotton cap on my round fat head, my eyes slits in my puffy face, my mouth open, as if a moment after the shutter clicked, I cried.

Well now here's something else to mark my godforsaken, good for nothing birthday—Cali's abduction and the annihilation of whatever trust in people she had left.

Chapter 46

Death is very likely the single best invention of life.

Steve Jobs

Gloria's vision was right about one thing—not the angels, but that Cali is in danger.

Where, exactly, are these people taking her? And if Elaine or Steve needed to or wanted to find her, could they?

Rita exits route 40 in Needles, then drives a short distance and stops the car. She opens the door and I see that she's parked between two RV's in the far end of a parking lot—is she trying to hide the car? Anyone looking for the Lincoln Town Car wouldn't look here. The sign on the funky yellow and brown restaurant says, "Covered Wagon Restaurant, Open 5:30 A.M. Daily."

Rita walks behind the car to Kirby's door, opens it and leans in.

"One of you needs to stay in the car with Miss Green." Rita says "Miss Green" with exaggerated formality.

Witt nods to Kirby. "Go ahead. I'm fine. But can you pick me up a large coffee—three sugars and two creamers—not cream or milk—but powdered creamers—and a sandwich? I don't care what kind as long as it doesn't have mustard."

What kind of person doesn't care what kind of sandwich he eats—and without mustard yet?

"Okay. Thanks," Kirby says as he jumps out of the car, then shuts the door, leaving Witt and Cali—as far as they know—alone in the back.

Cali's eyes open. She watches Kirby exit the car.

Now she squirms and incoherent sounds come through the wide piece of duct tape.

"If I were you, I'd just sit quietly," Witt says. "Rita might get really mad if I tell her you've been acting out."

The sounds that begin in Cali's throat get louder and she nods her head toward the restaurant. Rose jumps above the seat and floats above the place where Kirby sat.

"Hmm. I can't understand a word you're saying," Witless Witt says and then laughs at his own joke.

Cali squirms again and makes an urgent, incoherent sound. Rose growls.

Witt pushes his face very close to Cali's and places his big right hand on her left breast, fondles it for a moment, then squeezes it hard. "I said 'Sit still.'"

Pain reddens Cali's face. She stops moving and becomes silent.

"That's better," Witt says and laughs again, his hand dropping to her thigh.

Just then the passenger door opens. Witt lifts his hand quickly as Kirby leans in, a Styrofoam cup of coffee in one hand and a white paper bag in the other. "Here's your coffee and a tuna sandwich on rye. No mustard."

"Great," Witt says, putting the coffee and the bag on the floor. "I'm just going in to make a quick pit stop."

As Witt gets out, Kirby gets into the back seat. Then Rita appears and leans toward Cali from the open passenger door. Rita holds another white paper bag and a Styrofoam cup of water. "Although you haven't earned it, I am going to allow you to urinate."

Rita nods to Kirby. He releases Cali's seat belt, then pulls her elbow, guiding her out of the car. Rita opens the front passenger door and puts the white bag on the seat, the cup of water in the cup holder, then shuts the door.

Cali's legs are stiff. Her hands behind her back are pale beneath the metal handcuffs. Are they numb? Rita takes Cali's left elbow, Kirby her right. But instead of leading Cali inside the restaurant, Rita steers Cali to the left toward three large oak trees at the edge of the road along a chain link fence.

Rose and I follow.

Rita and Kirby stop when they reach the trees. Rita reaches over and unzips Cali's jeans, then pulls them down roughly. Then she pulls down Cali's underpants. Cali's eyes widen in embarrassment.

"Squat," Rita says, as she and Kirby release her elbows.

Cali hesitates, then squats and pees on the ground as Kirby and Rita stand beside her. Rita and Kirby then pull Cali quickly to her feet, tug on her underwear and zip her pants.

Jesus.

Rose tries to sniff the urine that sinks quickly into the sandy ground and gives me a puzzled look.

As Rita and Kirby hustle Cali back to the car, I look around, hoping someone sees Cali and call the police.

But Kirby tilts Cali's head down with his hand so that her long yellow hair obscures the duct tape on her mouth. If drivers passing by on Needles Highway or diners leaving the restaurant glance at Cali, they don't see a handcuffed girl being strong-armed. Instead they see a young carsick girl being helped back to into the car by her concerned parents and their friends.

Chapter 47

Vicki Petterson

After Needles it is Witt's turn to navigate the highway east toward Kingman, Arizona. The desert landscape is jagged blur behind the dark windows.

Rita wears a black sleep mask and dozes, her mouth open, her breathing slowing to lentissimo.

Kirby sips black coffee from the Styrofoam cup he holds in his right hand. Because Cali occupies the middle seat, the center console's cup holders are not available to him.

Cali is slumped in her seat, her head down. I hope she's asleep. They've been traveling about six or seven hours—when was the last time Cali had anything to drink? When they sedated her last night?

It could be twelve hours since she's had water.

The cup of water sits untouched in the front seat drink holder, strategically placed where Cali can see it. Whatever's in the white take-out bag remains on the floor near Rita's feet. Of course I can't smell it—nor can Rose—but I imagine that the scent of whatever the bag contains reaches Cali's nostrils each time she inhales.

Kirby glances at Rita then at Cali, whose eyes are fixed on the cup of water, the water's surface dimpling slightly from the car's vibration.

"Thirsty?" Kirby whispers into Cali's ear, then trails his fingers through her hair. I can see Witt glance into the rear view mirror and grin.

Cali opens her eyes and blinks, and turns her face away from Kirby's.

Kirby leans forward and removes the cup of water from the holder in the front, then holds it close to Cali's duct taped mouth.

"Thirsty?" he whispers again.

Cali avoids his eyes, then suddenly lifts her right knee in an attempt to knock the cup out of Kirby's hand—but Kirby is too quick and pulls cup away before it spills.

Cali's sudden movement disturbs Rita.

Rita pulls the sleep mask off her head in time to observe Kirby returning the cup of water to the front seat drink holder.

"Give it to me," she says, frowning. Kirby looks sheepish as he retracts his hand and gives the cup to Rita's outstretched one. "Take off the tape."

With his left palm, Kirby pushes Cali's head against the seat. As he pulls the tape from Cali's mouth, it makes a sound like fabric ripping.

Cali's lips and the skin around her mouth are raw. She licks her lips tentatively with her tongue.

"Give her water," Rita instructs Kirby. He takes the cup from the front and tilts it to Cali's mouth. Cali gulps the water down quickly.

"Thank you," Cali says—her voice is hoarse—but this horrifies me—she sounds sincerely grateful—"Thank you," she says again.

I can't stand listening to Cali thank these shits for anything.

Rita takes the paper bag from the car floor and opens it, and lifts out a small Styrofoam container and a black plastic spoon. She pulls off the lid to reveal about a cup of cooked white rice.

"Feed her," Rita says to Kirby, then pulls the sleep mask over her eyes, turns toward the dark window, once again relaxes into an untroubled sleep.

Chapter 48

"Death is one of the few things that can be done as easily lying down."

Woody Allen

A half a cup of cold, gelatinous white rice and a few swallows of water. Duct tape. Handcuffs. Peeing on the ground.

Where did these people learn this crap? At a boarding school?

I know that Rita referred to Kirby and Witt as an "extraction team" when she spoke to Elaine and Steve. I'm sure the technical and important-sounding term wowed Elaine and she didn't think at all about what "extraction team" might actually mean.

Well now I know that this extraction business is not just about securely moving a troubled, erratic child from one location to another—it's about intimidation and breaking a child's will. And the downcast and obsequious way Cali thanks Kirby for a few sips of water and rice is proof that their cruelty works.

Kirby drives until he stops in Kingman at a gas station. Rita uses the restroom and then goes into the station's mini-mart. She returns to the car with fresh coffee and a brown bag from which she removes some candy bars and a package of mini-doughnuts and places them on the front passenger seat. Then Witt gets out and Rita reclaims the driver's seat. After Witt returns, he gets in the back next to Cali and Kirby takes his turn.

Cali is quiet all the way to Albuquerque though her mouth is still free of duct tape. She does not complain that the handcuffs hurt her hands or that her shoulders ache. She does not ask for food or water or to stop the car so that she can urinate. Instead she watches like a cat through half-closed eyes as Rita, Kirby and Witt sip their beverages and eat their snacks.

And Rose watches Cali, her eyes wide and mournful.

Rita exits the highway in Rio Rancho—I follow the car's route on the re-animated navigation screen—then drives a few minutes and stops the car.

When she opens the door I can see that she's parked on a narrow road with desert on both sides.

"Get her out," Rita says.

Kirby releases Cali's seat belt and gets out of the car. Witt exits and walks to Kirby's side. They both watch Cali as she slides out of the back seat.

Rose sails out after Cali and I—like a puff of stale air—flow invisible into the night.

The darkness is massive and deep. Swirls of stars dangle above us like frozen fireworks. In the distance a rectangular mountain range is visible as a deeper and unbroken blackness in the sky. If there is sage and piñon in the dry air, I can't smell them—but I can tell it's cold from the puffs of breath above Rita's, Cali's Witt and Kirby's living mouths.

Same drill. They let Cali pee, then rush her back into the car and secure her seat belt.

Rita drives purposefully into the dark for another hour or so, then pulls off the highway and drives for a short time before she parks the car on a street. Outside the car I see we're just off a plaza in front of an adobe building with a number of offices within it—Taos Bootery and Shoe Repair, Kiva Children's Dentistry, Adobe Boba and Smoothies, Taos Tax Preparation, Kottonwood Koffee, Roca Azul Gallery, Roadrunner Nails and Serene Mountain Retreat.

Lights are on in the Serene Mountain office. Rita gets out of the car and goes around to the trunk, where she removes the duffel bag. Kirby gets out next, then Cali and Witt.

Rita leads the way to the turquoise blue door marked with a brown wooden sign that says "Serene Mountain Retreat." Witt and Kirby flank Cali. Their footsteps seem loud on the stone path.

Rita opens the door and Rose and I follow the foursome inside to a small reception area decorated in Southwest style--red tile floor, wood and leather chairs arranged around a rustic table, hunting trophies—an elk head and one of a coyote--with glass eyes and shiny teeth—and a string of red chilies hanging on one wall next to a glass display case with Indian pots, arrowheads, and baskets. I can't tell if the Indian stuff is real, but the chilies are plastic.

Brochures like the one Rita gave Elaine sit in a neat pile on the table next to a phallic cactus in a ceramic pot.

A large bulletin board decorates the other wall. On it are what look like stock color photographs of teenagers hiking, cooking around a campfire, skiing, setting up a tent, and standing on the summit of a mountain. A door next to the bulletin board opens and a tall, rugged man in his forties strides out of an inner office in which I see a big desk covered with papers, file cabinets, a desktop computer and a printer.

"Rita," the man says warmly. "You made great time."

"Thanks, Bruce," Rita says. "I did my best. You'll find everything in here," Rita says, "tuition and the rest." Rita hands Bruce the duffel. He tosses it inside his office and closes the door.

"Good," Bruce says and smiles. Then he looks at Cali.

Cali looks bedraggled and small. She stands between Kirby and Witt, her hands still cuffed, her lips raw and her eyes focused on the floor. "And you must be Cali," Bruce says as if he's meeting a debutante at a cocktail party. "It's wonderful to finally meet you."

Cali says nothing.

"Gentlemen," Bruce continues, "It's time Cali was more comfortable, don't you think?"

Witt fishes the handcuff key from his pocket and unlocks the cuffs. Cali's arms drop to her sides and she rubs her hands and wrists as if they're frozen.

"I apologize for the handcuffs, Cali," Bruce says in a kindly voice. "And for any discomfort you might have experienced during your transition from home."

Fear and fury blacken the blue of Cali's pupils, but she says nothing.

"Are you hungry or thirsty?" Bruce continues. He's wearing blue jeans, a blue work shirt, brown cowboy boots and a brown sweater—he looks like he stepped right out of the Sundance catalogue.

"I'm hungry," Cali whispers. "And thirsty."

Bruce opens the door to his office, ducks inside, and reappears carrying two granola bars and a plastic bottle of water. Cali receives them eagerly, tears open a bar, and begins to eat.

"When do you expect Nora, John and Parvati?" Rita asks Bruce. She is sitting in one of the chairs now and studying her cell phone.

"They're on their way," Bruce says as if this is very happy news.

Cali has opened the second granola bar, bites off a big piece, and chews it intently.

"Cali," Bruce says, "I know you're tired and confused. But you need to realize that the only thing that stands between you and jail is your new school. A new and important chapter of your life is starting. And it's extremely important that you begin on the right foot."

And with the right clichés. I hate this motivational shit.

Cali looks frankly at Bruce, swallowing the last bite of the second bar and asks, "Who are you?"

Chapter 49

"When one man dies, one chapter is not torn out of the book, but translated into a better language."

John Donne

Bruce chuckles as if Cali has said something funny. "I'm Bruce Bennion, Cali. The director of your new school, Serene Mountain Retreat. I should have introduced myself before."

Cali takes a gulp of water and waits for Bennion to say more.

Bennion is silent.

Cali swallows the last chunk of granola bar. "This is the school?" Cali asks looking skeptically around the small office.

Kirby and Witt laugh until Bennion's frown silences them.

"Ours is a therapeutic wilderness program, Cali. You'll be spending most of your time outdoors. This is our administrative center."

He forgot to say "state of the art," didn't he?

The door opens. A blond woman in her twenties enters, then a lanky man in overalls and a young woman with long dark hair braided into a ponytail. They're all dressed in winter clothes.

"Nora. John. Parvati," Bruce says. "You're here."

We can all see that they're here, Bruce old buddy.

Rose has tired of the cactus and sits at attention next to Cali's feet, studying the new people in the room.

The small office feels crowded. Rita gets up from the chair.

"This is Cali. Cali Green," Bruce explains to the trio. "Cali, come meet your new best friends—Nora, John and Parvati."

On cue Nora, John and Parvati smile at Cali.

Cali doesn't smile back.

"They're going to supervise your orientation and adjustment period," Bennion smiles. "Now I'm going to be up front with you, Cali. It's not going to be easy. You're going to start at the very bottom and have to work your way up. Every privilege at Serene Mountain must be earned."

Cali looks skeptical, but Bennion persists, "And this is the best part, Cali. Your orientation begins right now."

Chapter 50

*"All living things were brothers, and all dead things were even more
so."*

Kurt Vonnegut

After the long ride and the mock formality of the office,
everything speeds up.

Nora takes Cali's hand. Parvati puts her arm around
Cali's shoulder. John moves behind Cali.

Witt and Kirby stand with Bennion and watch the three
young people—without discernable force or effort—quickly
maneuver Cali out the office door. They remind me of those
hucksters who seem to bend spoons with their fingertips or
appear to levitate.

Rose and I can levitate and so we do—right through
Witt, Kirby, Rita and Bruce and out the door, across the
gravel and into a dusty and mud-spattered black pickup truck
with narrow back seat behind the driver and passenger seat.
Like the Town Car, its windows are tinted, but they're not
quite as dark.

Parvati drives out of Taos and onto what must be a
highway. Nora and John sit in the back with Cali in the
middle. No one speaks. Once again the darkened windows
obscure the view, but after about forty minutes the road gets
rough and the truck seems to be climbing.

After about fifteen minutes more and a series of turns,
the truck stops. Parvati leaves the headlights on while she
gets out and goes to the back of the truck.

John hops out and motions to Cali to follow.

Nora is the last one out. She leads Cali a few feet ahead of the vehicle and tells her to stay where she is. The lights both illuminate and blind Cali, and reveal a rutted Martian-red dirt road with dark scrub and trees beyond.

"Take off your clothes," Nora instructs Cali.

"What?" Cali blinks in the bright light. "Here? It's freezing."

It's good to finally hear Cali's voice again, even though her voice is hoarse—I worried that Cali was disappearing into herself.

"One thing you've got to learn, maggot," Parvati says, placing emphasis on "maggot," "is that you do what you're told. Now strip."

I am so angry that I forget what and who I am and place myself between Cali and Parvati.

But I cannot shield Cali from what happens next.

Cali shakes her head ever so slightly, but she drops to the ground and slowly unties her tennis shoes. She pulls off her socks—also slowly— then stands again and unzips her jeans and removes them. Then she turns her back to the headlights and lifts her sweatshirt and the t-shirt underneath over her head. She turns around in her bra and underpants, shivering. The headlights bleach her pale skin of color and turn the scene high-contrast black and white.

"Come on, maggot," Parvati says. "Stop wasting my time."

Cali removes her bra and panties and stands blinking in the bright light, her cheeks flushing and her body shaking.

"Drug check," Nora says cheerfully. "Bend over, maggot."

John walks toward carrying a flashlight and Cali bends over.

Parvati stands behind Cali while John shines the flashlight on her buttocks. Nora puts on a latex glove and quickly probes her—Cali cries out.

"Okay, maggot," Nora says. "Open you mouth." John shines the flashlight into Cali's mouth and nostrils for Nora's inspection.

"You can get dressed now, maggot," Nora says and walks back to the truck.

Cali quickly covers herself with the pile of clothing on the ground and dresses hastily, then takes a step or two toward the truck.

"Did anyone say you could move, maggot?" Nora asks.

Cali stands still.

Do I hear dogs barking in the distance? I can't tell, but Rose's ears swivel and she opens her mouth halfway, as if she's trying to taste the air.

"That's better, maggot," Nora says. "We're not quite done with you."

Parvati produces a pair of scissors from her jacket, then grabs Cali's long hair into one handful and cuts. The handful of yellow hair shines silver in the bluish headlights as it scatters on the rocky ground.

Rose floats into Cali's elongated shadow, which looks like a silhouette of a man on stilts.

"But why?" Cali says to Parvati, the anger gone now.

"Because maggots are ugly," Parvati says. "Now get back into the truck."

Cali touches the newly bare nape of her neck and her jagged jaw-length hair, then walks slowly to the truck.

"Move!" Parvati orders, holding the truck's door open, "Unless you want to crawl."

Cali quickens her pace. But when she reaches the truck's door, she slows and looks at Parvati straight on, "I don't care what you do to me or how long it takes. I'm going to get away from you."

Chapter 51

"We're born, we live a little while, we die."

E.B. White

I don't know if Rose and I imperceptibly deaden more and more, or remain as we are—which is pretty fucking dead, thank you very much—but I do know that things in the living world can always get worse.

Rose does the post-mortal equivalent of a headstand.

She lingers motionless—paws and head down, back legs and tail up--relaxed—absolutely nothing sustaining or steadying her position or her altitude—her eyes looking into mine.

I scratch Rose's barrel chest, then stroke the soft fur behind her ears.

We've returned to the afterlife so I can clear my head— and maybe figure some things out.

My meditation is not philosophically ambitious. I've given up hoping that death would transfigure or improve me—even my hair and fingernails have failed to grow.

I've stopped trying to understand where my big fat dead ass fits into the cosmos.

Or why a guy on a bicycle shot me to death as I walked home with a to-go order of warm fried chicken and waffles in a paper bag.

Or why the seamless wall dividing life and death appears to have developed cracks.

Rose blinks.

How do Rose and I help Cali now?

How do we free the Beverly Hills One?

We were with Cali when she got back in the truck and Nora navigated it along increasingly narrow and rough roads until she finally stopped outside a high, chain-link gate. Parvati got out and pushed the gate open, then waited for the truck to pass. As it did, its headlights swept across silvery quivering aspens and a carved wooden sign:

SERENE SUMMIT RETREAT
At ROCA AZUL
PRIVATE
TRESPASSERS WILL BE PROSECUTED

Rose and I trespassed—as the truck wobbled along a narrow road that ended at an A-frame wooden building.

Parvati and John, carrying flashlights, led Cali past the A-frame to a small, low-roofed, windowless building in the back.

We followed Cali and the beam of Parvati's flashlight as it swept low metal cots lined up along the walls, thin army surplus green blankets covering angular human shapes, and a row of white plastic buckets filled with water in the corner, a ladle hanging from each one.

I counted the buckets and then I counted the cots. There was one bucket for each cot.

Parvati let her flashlight's beam fall upon an empty cot in the corner and nodded at Cali.

Cali understood. She walked into the light and then out of it back into the dark to reach the bed and then sits down.

Rose and I watched Parvati leave.

We saw a dozen pairs of eyes opened then, the whites gleaming in the darkness as they stared at Cali. We watched Cali turn away, wrap herself in the thin blanket and curl up facing the wall.

Chapter 52

All I know is that we can't help Cali from the other side

So Rose and I float above Cali's cot. The sky is just beginning to lighten. Is Cali sleeping? I can't tell.

Nora enters, blowing a shrill whistle. "Get up, maggots!"

Cali and the other kids rise from their cots. In the light I can see how skinny they are—boys and girls from maybe thirteen to maybe seventeen—with dirty faces and black fingernails. Some slide their filthy bare feet into flip-flops and wrap their army blankets around their shoulders. Others, like Cali, have tennis shoes and socks.

We watch as the young people file out of the small building and shuffle to an area behind the A frame building where three Dumpsters are secured with padlocks.

Parvati, in a red down jacket and wool cap—it must be cold—waits for them.

"The maggots may feed," Parvati says ceremoniously as she unlocks the padlocks on the dumpsters.

What the fuck?

The kids, with Cali a few steps behind, ignore the Dumpsters. Instead they rush through a door that leads inside the A-frame and enter a kitchen with wide stainless steel counters and appliances. A few dirty breakfast dishes and cups and glasses are piled into two large sinks.

These dishes must belong to Parvati, John and Nora.

Cali freezes when she sees what happens next--the kids fight over the remaining bits of food, elbowing each other away from the cups half full of juice or milk.

"You'd better hurry, Cali," Parvati says, "Or you'll be a very hungry maggot."

Cali stares at Parvati, then runs to the sink and grabs a crust of toast from a plate half-immersed in gray, soapy water.

When the few stomach-turning bits of leftover food are gone, a tall boy begins rinsing the dishes while a tiny girl in flip-flops loads them into a large dishwasher. Other kids sweep the floor, wipe down the counters and take out the trash in large garbage bags to the Dumpsters, which Parvati locks once again.

Did Parvati padlock them because of wild animals? Or to keep hungry kids from rummaging for food?

I decide to check out the property.

As we move around, I realize that Rose has never been in a wild place before. Her eyes follow the trajectories of birds and clouds, and her ears stiffen at the sounds the wind carries through the quiet.

It's weird how quiet it is here.

Not once do I hear the young people speak. They are silent while Parvati lines them up and marches them up a rocky path to a clearing interrupted by tree stumps and rocks and boulders of various sizes. Mute, the young people work with picks and shovels and their hands to dig out the stumps, or to push the sometimes very heavy boulders under the trees.

Is this supposed to be character building, hazing or just forced labor?

I vote for number three. I suspect that shit Bennion needs a new parking lot.

Every so often Parvati announces in a loud voice, "Maggots work in the dirt."

This goes on for an hour or so. Nervous, Rose stays close to Cali as she works.
Then John appears and marches the kids back down the path to the area by the Dumpsters once again.

One boy lags behind. I can't tell if he is ill, or just hungry and dehydrated. He's Asian with a slight build and looks around thirteen.

John looks back at him, annoyed. "Gary, move it! Or you'll miss lunch again."

Gary tries to move faster, but is still much slower than the rest. I move to the back of the line of young people and see why: One of Gary's flip-flops is gone and he walks with one bare foot on the uneven path.

By the time Gary makes it back, the kids are sitting on the ground in a circle—some on their haunches and some cross-legged—waiting like feral cats for food, their eyes on the kitchen door.

Cali keeps rubbing her forehead and squinting her eyes. How high up is this place, I wonder. I remember visiting Santa Fe years ago and getting a nasty headache while my body adjusted to the altitude.

Parvati finally opens the kitchen door and carries a large aluminum pot, which she places on the ground in the middle of the circle.

The pot contains a lumpy mixture of white rice and scraps—gray pieces of meat or chicken, some yellow flecks that could be egg, and a few red beans.

Parvati waits for what seems like at least two long minutes before she says, " "Eat, maggots."

That's when the kids—Cali, too—dig into the pot with their bare and dirty hands, greedily taking handfuls of the rice mixture and shoving them into their mouths.

Chapter 53

"Death must be so beautiful. . . To forget time, to forgive life, to be at peace."

Oscar Wilde

State of the art my ass.

Therapeutic my ass.

The place is total bullshit.

A fraud.

Nothing remotely resembles a "retreat"—whatever the fuck that is—or a school. While the kids finish eating their slop, Rose and I enter the A frame building.

Inside is a small kitchen—well stocked with food--a small office with a telephone and a computer, a television, a bathroom and three small rooms where I assume that Parvati, John and Nora sleep.

Nowhere do I see even one book.

No fucking way Parvati, John and Nora are teachers. Or psychologists.

I hate everything I see. And I wonder what Bruce Bennion is really up to.

I hear John's voice and we return to the area behind the Dumpsters.

"Maggots, arrange yourselves in three lines."

The kids do as they are told.

"One hundred jumping jacks, maggots!" John yells. "One, two, three…"

The kids jump in time to John's commands. But I can see Gary is struggling.

Parvati walks to him and puts her hand on his shoulder. "Come with me you lazy maggot," she orders.

Gary, breathless and ashamed, and Rose and I follow Parvati up the path to the area where the rocks and boulders were being cleared earlier. The sun is very high now and very bright.

"One hundred sit-ups, maggot!" Parvati orders.

Gary drops to the ground and begins to do the sit-ups as Parvati counts down from one hundred.

I can't watch. And I wish I could cover my ears. Gary groans and gasps with the exertion, moving more slowly and painfully with each crunch.

"Come on, maggot!" Parvati urges him. "Or you'll have to do two hundred."

I look away and see the one thing that matches Bennion's bullshit brochure—a mountain visible from this clearing in the distance, a few rough patches of snow glowing neon blue on its contours as the sun sinks slowly into the afternoon sky.

So that must be Roca Azul—the blue mountain.

Chapter 54

"A dead man is the best fall guy in the world. He never talks back."

Raymond Chandler

I'm going to find out how Bennion gets away with this shit—I was going to add "If it kills me"—but I stop myself.

Things are going on that I can't see. I'm sure of that.

The first place to check is the Serene Mountain Retreat office.

Rose and I pass through the exterior wall and find the reception area empty. Bennion must be in the back office. We float into a small workspace.

It has southwestern touches, just like the front. Kachina dolls. Pottery. Bowls, mostly—some shiny black and some with black designs on beige clay.

A calendar on the wall above Bennion's desk has a picture of a German shepherd or a coyote howling at a full moon among craggy rocks and pine trees. Red X's have been drawn inside the boxes ending at October 25.

Bennion, in another Sundance Catalogue-worthy outfit, sits behind his desk typing quickly at a computer. Next to the keyboard is a tall "Kottonwood Koffee, Taos, N.M." take-out cup—more southwestern bullshit. Next to the cup sits a plump—and probably state of the art—glazed donut on a paper napkin. The doughnut is golden and puffy. The glaze is thin and reflective—like thin ice.

I look away from the perfect and eternally inaccessible doughnut and check out the computer screen. Bennion inserts text into a template with the title, "Orientation Assessment: Cali Green. 11/20."

Wait.

Doesn't the dog calendar say that it's October?

"Cali's transition from home to school has progressed smoothly. I am pleased to inform you that she is making appropriate progress through the orientation process."

Bennion stops to take a bite out of the doughnut.

A glistening tear-shaped drop of raspberry jelly falls from the doughnut's soft interior to Bennion's bottom lip, but he doesn't notice. Before I can stop myself, my dry tongue touches my own cracked lip—searching for a phantom jewel-like jelly blob I can neither taste nor smell.

Bennion reads over the text he's just typed, nods and types some more.

"Cali is responding well to group therapy sessions with our staff psychologist, but we wish she would be a little less reticent about her feelings." Bennion stops and takes a swig of his coffee.

"Cali has begun to accept that many of her issues involve misplaced anger. We and our psychiatric staff look forward to working more on her anger issues with Cali in the coming months. Although school staff has repeatedly given Cali the opportunity to phone home, she has not availed herself of this opportunity. We hope you understand that her decision is not a reflection of her feelings toward you. Please be advised that withdrawal from family is normal and can indicate Cali has begun to feel shame and regret for her past inappropriate behaviors. Cali is bonding successfully with school staff and her fellow students and I am confident that she will contribute a great deal to our school."

What a wordy, lying son of a bitch. Elaine will be impressed.

Near the printer on a small table is a stack of papers that look like the one on the computer screen. I wish I could pick them up and read through them, but I cannot.

I content myself with scanning the page on top: "Eric is responding well to group therapy sessions with our psychiatrist, but we wish he would be a little less reticent about his feelings. But Eric has begun to accept that his episodes of acting out involved misplaced anger. Psychiatric staff look forward to working on this issue with Eric in the coming months."

Bennion has reached the "Academic Progress" box now on the computer screen: "Cali is keeping up with her work overall and her academic progress has been satisfactory despite having fallen behind on a few occasions in mathematics and history. Literature and U.S. Government are her favorite classes. "

Bennion types fast and hits the tab key. The cursor jumps to the final box, "Therapeutic Wilderness Program": "I am very happy to report that our therapeutic wilderness program is particularly effective for Cali, who hikes daily and makes the most of her time outdoors. Cali responds well to the pristine natural environment Serene Mountain Retreat affords and is becoming physically stronger, more independent and more able to reflect upon her life and her future goals."

I'm sure Eric—whichever cold, skinny, hungry dirty kid he is—reflects often on his goals, too—the primary ones being eating a hot meal and getting the fuck out of Bruce Bennion's bogus school for which Eric's parents are probably bleeding—like Elaine and Steve—six or seven grand a month.

Jesus.

When you deduct the three bucks a week Bennion must spend on each kid's food—and whatever he's paying Parvati, Nora and John and had to pay Witt and Kirby to drag the kids here—his Serene Mountain School is hauling in an avalanche of cash.

Chapter 55

"Nothing can happen more beautiful than death."

Walt Whitman

Rose barks and I follow her into the reception area. After lumbering over the earth for thirty-eight years, death's frictionless mobility still surprises me.

Rita enters the office carrying a package of manila envelopes. Her cheeks are flushed from the cold and her hair has frizzed into an orange froth around her head.

When I said she looked like a Hummel figurine, I was wrong. She looks exactly like a grown up Campbell's Soup Kid—big head, red cheeks, and curls.

"It's me," she says and stops to straighten the pile of school brochures on the table. "I picked up the envelopes for the progress reports."

Rita takes off her down jacket and gloves and tosses them on the couch, then enters Bennion's office.

"Thanks," he says and clicks "print." "But remember not to mail them until after the twentieth."

"Okay, right," Rita says.

The printer spits out pages. Rita gathers them and reads the one on top. "Her parents will eat up this stuff. You should have seen all the books they have in their library."

What does she expect in a library? Hats?

"And all the antiques," she adds.

Elaine would be pleased to know that her tsotchkes and faux first editions had the effect she desired on this sociopathic guest to her gracious mega-home. Except Rita's belief that the fake tomes are valuable will only make Bennion want to keep Cali as long as he possibly can.

This is not good news. I don't think that oppositional and defiant Cali could survive a winter here.

"How are the happy campers?" Bennion asks.

"Miserable," Rita says. "Especially Gary Chung and Cali Green. Gary's just a loser. But Parvati says the Green girl is a spoiled little bitch. You know the type—she seems to think that her shit doesn't smell."

"Well, Parvati will disabuse her of that notion soon," Bennion chuckles.

What a pompous schmuck. Who the fuck talks like this? How I wish I could disabuse him of his verticality and knock him and Rita face first into the dumpster.

A soup kid laugh escapes from Rita's rosebud mouth. "The new parking area is almost cleared."

"That was fast," Bennion says.

"Nora decided that's pretty much all the kids should be doing. And I think it was a good idea," Rita adds.

"Good. Good work. I have a small project of my own to complete. I should have it finished before the kids return from The Seeking."

Chapter 56

"Life is but a dream for the dead."

Gerard Way

Rose and I follow Bennion out of the office and down the street. He walks like the Marlboro Man after an especially good day on the range—confident, graceful, straight and strong despite smoking six packs a day.

I make a bet with myself that Bennion is going to the bank to deposit some of the checks he's receiving from parents to subsidize the misery of kids like Cali.

But his pace doesn't slow until he reaches a small art gallery. A small printed card on the door says, "Art Opening Today: The Many Moods of Roca Azul by Wish Feather."

Bennion enters.

Rose and I pass through the glass window into the gallery.

Mostly middle-aged and older people stand around holding plastic cups of white wine. Most are dressed like Bennion—Sundance catalogue meets Barney's. Lots of leather, embroidery, embellishments and cashmere. The women wear heavy silver and turquoise necklaces, earrings and rings. Some of the men wear bolos with silver and inlaid designs.

A recording of Native American chants plays softly on a hidden speaker.

My father wore western clothing for his TV show—blue jeans, boots, a red and yellow plaid shirt with white snaps, a brown cowboy hat and a red bandana around his neck. He never wore stuff like this. These people are loaded.

One woman has more jewelry than the rest. She has short gray hair and freckles, and wears a beaded fringe vest over a red dress. She stands in the center of a group of admirers. This woman, I gather, is Wish Feather. Her paintings cover the walls—large oils thickly applied evoking sunsets behind Roca Azul that burn as bright as a nuclear conflagration.

Kachinas and tightly woven baskets sit inside Plexiglas cases on white rectangular pedestals. As the art lovers admire them, Wish Feather's paintings and some beige and black ceramic pots, Bennion moves easily from one group to another.

Rose floats next to me, but then pauses above one of the Kachinas. She drops close to the carved and decorated figure and tries to sniff the gray fur on its mask. I look more closely and see that the figure wears a dog-faced mask. A small card says, "Traditional Carved Poko (Dog) Kachina."

Bennion stops schmoozing and steps to the back of the gallery, nodding at a pretty young woman with long black hair who sits behind a desk.

Then he opens a door marked "No Admittance," and enters a storage area.

Bennion clearly knows his way around. Is he part owner this place?

Rose and I follow Bennion through the door.

Chapter 57

"For death begins with life's first breath."

John Oxenham

The gallery's back room is large. Humming fluorescent lights give a green tinge to the white walls, concrete floor, and a jumble of crates, cardboard boxes and industrial tables. On them are piled Navajo blankets, sand-gray and red. Heaps of silver and turquoise jewelry. Cradleboards. Arrowheads. A real treasure hoard if you like this kind of stuff.

I don't.

Bennion makes his way around the boxes until he stands near a thirty-ish woman with wavy brown hair pulled back in a long pony tail. She is not dressed for the art opening. Instead she wears jeans, scuffed cowboy boots, and a faded blue sweatshirt.

The woman wraps a beige and black pottery bowl in large sheets of bubble wrap. "Bruce."

"Rebecca," Bennion says. He strides close to the table and nudges and moves the bubble wrap. Then, to Rose's discomfort, he whistles in admiration.

"May I?" But Bennion doesn't wait for Rebecca to give him permission to touch the bowl. He lifts it with both hands and slowly turns it slowly to examine the design.

Rebecca stands back and watches, her narrow lips curving into a smile.

"Incredible, isn't it?" she asks. "I can't believe I was able to get my hands on a Nampeyo jar. I have two collectors in Paris fighting over it right now. It's one of the most valuable pieces I've ever acquired. "

"Yes. I believe it is," Bennion says. "But not the most valuable. Not by a long shot."

"Oh really?" Rebecca gently takes the jar from Bennion and resumes wrapping the jar.

"Yes. Really." Bennion ceremoniously removes a small piece of tissue paper from his pocket and hands it to Rebecca.

Inside the tissue is a curved, drab shard of broken pottery. Rebecca's eyes widen as she looks at the object.

"I can't believe it, Bruce. You finally hit pay dirt. Am I holding what I think I'm holding? " Rebecca lightly and slowly traces the shard's curve with her finger.

Bruce grins. "It's from a bowl. With a kill hole. And there are pots that appear intact."

I waft close to see the object in Rebecca's hand, and Rose follows me.

What's the big deal? It's just a piece of a broken clay pot.

What is Rebecca so excited about?

But the shard disturbs Rose. She recoils, stares at Rebecca and Bennion, and releases a deep, and angry growl.

Chapter 58

"From a proud tower in the town
Death looks gigantically down..."

Edgar Allan Poe

It is the middle of the night. Sorry. But that's all I can tell you. There are no clocks here—perhaps this is Bennion's way of disorienting the kids more than they already are.

Ashen moonlight spills through the window near where Cali sleeps under her thin blanket.

Rose and I linger like incense in the darkness above her.

Watching. Waiting.

What was so important about that piece of pottery in the gallery? It didn't look like much. And it was not even decorated.

And why did it bother Rose?

I have no fucking idea except that if it upsets Rose, it can't be good.

And what did Bennion and Nora mean when they talked about The Seeking?

The Seeking sounds ominous—like the scary part of a Madeleine L'Engle novel or something cult members are made to do after their leaders become psychotic.

Seeking what?

Something that benefits Bennion, I'm sure of that. The Seeking could mean almost anything unpleasant in a place where kids eat garbage and are forced to drag rocks around all day.

And Bennion's "project"? What is it?

A canine howl from somewhere high on the mountain interrupts my thoughts and causes Rose to cock her head.

Rose howls in answer, a long, high-pitched call. There's a moment of silence and then distant howls, yips and barks fill the night.

The door to the A frame opens and the icy beam of an LED flashlight cuts through the night.

Parvati and John.

They move to the cot in the corner and shake its occupant. As Parvati's flashlight sweeps over him, I see Gary blink in fear and confusion.

"Come with us," Parvati orders and clicks off the flashlight.

Gary scrambles off his cot as Parvati steps toward Cali.

"Cali Green," Parvati says and angles the flashlight in her face. Cali blinks.

"Yes." Cali says very quietly.

"Come with us."

Cali slips on her tennis shoes and gets out of the bed, the blanket still around her shoulders. The others watch as she follows Gary, Parvati and John outside and disappears into the darkness.

Parvati and John seem so comfortable, so confident in the dark.

They do not know a ghostly dog drifts close to Cali. And they do not see what I have become—an angry, vengeful ghost.

Chapter 59

"How wonderful is Death!"

Percy Bysshe Shelley

Parvati and John urge Cali and Gary along the path. The only sound is the gravel crunching under John and Parvati's boots and the soft thwap of Cali's sneakers.

Gary's bare feet are noiseless.

The coyotes have settled down. Only the wind hisses now and then in the trees.

Well, look who's here.

Bennion waits at the Dumpsters.

He wears a headlamp with a small, blinding LED beam. I think I saw one like it in my shit brother's Hammacher-Schlemmer catalogue for four hundred and fifty bucks.

Only the best for Bruce fucking Bennion.

He lets Cali and Gary stand awkwardly for few moments—just to intensify their discomfort.

"Life is not a rehearsal," Bennion finally intones, aiming his headlamp beam into the darkness to illustrate how fragile life—light, get it?—is and how easily obliterated. "Your future starts right now. The stakes are high. What happens next will be completely up to you."

Gary coughs and hugs himself. Cali is quiet, but I see that she's trembling—from fear, or from the cold, or both.

Not more this motivational crap, I silently beg. But the jerk can't help himself.

"Today is the first day of the rest of your life!" Bennion pauses to let this mock-profundity sink into Cali's and Gary's heads.

Rose whines and places herself between Bennion and Cali.

"This school, Cali and Gary, is all that protects you both from a long and ugly period of incarceration."

Melodramatic pause.

"Jail," Bennion continues. "And a record that will destroy your prospects for the rest of your lives. In other words, this school is your last chance."

Another pause while Bennion looks above Cali and Gary into the darkness overtaking his flashlight's beam and then says, "Yet school staff informs me that neither of you fully grasps this very important truth."

Gary is quiet.

Cali looks at Bennion and says, "But this isn't a school."

I want to cheer, to whistle, to hug Cali for having the chutzpah to spit the right truth back at this asshole.

Bennion's quick blow knocks Cali to the ground and shocks her into silence.

Rose barks as if she had been the one to feel it—or perhaps the memory of being hit is indelible.

Gary kneels next to Cali and murmurs something. Cali holds her hand to the the side of her face that Bennion smacked. She's been thrown to her knees in the gravel and she remains there, making herself small.

Bennion shines the flashlight's cold light into Cali's face. "Get up. Now. You too, Gary."

Gary stands and coughs again. He's breathing heavily. Cali gets to her feet, bending down quickly to retrieve the blanket.

"That was to demonstrate to you some of the pain that you've caused your parents, Miss Green. And there's more where that came from—" Bennion slaps her face again, his hand open, but this time Cali fights the impact and remains upright.

Rose whimpers.

Gary rushes toward Bennion and tries to hit him. He's pathetic. Ridiculous. Brave.

Bennion swats Gary away as John grabs him in a chokehold and forces him to the ground.

Gary struggles and begins to gasp. "Let go! I'm choking!"

"You're talking, aren't you?" John taunts. "You're just fine."

"Because here. At this school." Bennion pauses for a moment after "school" apparently unaware of the irony of making such a pronouncement in the middle of fucking nowhere behind some Dumpsters as a young boy is being tortured, "you are held accountable for your actions. For your disrespectful attitude."

Bennion turns toward Cali. She closes her eyes to shut out the light of his headlamp, or to stop the tears from coming. "For your selfishness," Bennion continues. "For your ugliness. For your complete and utter worthlessness. And most of all," Bennion hits her again across her face again as if to punctuate his speech, "for your ingratitude."

Chapter 60

"It seems to me that one ought to rejoice in the fact of death."

James Baldwin

John has Gary pinned to the ground.

The only sounds are the wheezes coming from Gary's chest.

Parvati shines her flashlight on Gary. His small chest heaves, his brows are furrowed and he gasps for air. The terror in Gary's eyes is real.

"I'm--choking!" Gary wheezes.

John and Parvati exchange a look. "If you can talk, you're not choking," John insists.

"Get up! Stop faking, you little queer." Bennion shouts.

Rose moves close to Gary as a spasm travels through Gary's chest and body. She stays with him when his body becomes still and quiet.

John releases his hold and looks at Parvati and Bennion. "He's kidding, right?"

"Gary!" Parvati shouts, as she drops to the gravel beside him and slaps his face. "Gary!"

Chapter 61

"This ... Is the overnight endless trip to the famous unfathomable abyss."

Delmore Schwartz

John lifts Gary's limp body from the ground.

"Is Gary okay?" Cali asks, her voice husky.

"He's fine. He just needs some medication," Bennion says quickly. "Go back to your cabin now and stay there. And don't tell the others that Gary is sick. Do you understand? There's no point worrying them about nothing."

Cali nods and disappears as instructed in the direction of the cabin.

Bennion grimaces and then nods toward John and Parvati. "Take him into the office."

They walk to the A-frame in silence.

Parvati opens the door for John and switches on the overhead light. Bennion follows John inside.

John places Gary's floppy body on the floor and presses his ear to Gary's mouth.

Parvati knocks loudly on one of the bedroom doors.

"Nora! Wake up!"

Bennion remains standing. "Is he breathing?"

"I'm not sure," John says.

"Shit!" Parvati says.

"We have to do CPR," John says.

Nora emerges from her room rubbing her eyes. "What happened?"

"We don't know," Bennion lies, and looks meaningfully first at Parvati, then at John. "He just stopped breathing."

John lifts Gary's loose sweatshirt to expose his chest, and begins to apply a series of compressions with cupped hands, right under Gary's sternum.

Gary's body shudders with the force of each compression. Rose recoils each time, but stays close , floating right above Gary's heart.

After what seem like many minutes of exertion John stops.

There is no sputter or even a sigh from Gary.

His lips turn gray, then blue.

Then an enormous and leaden silence engulfs us—Gary, Bennion, Parvati, John, Nora, Rose and me.

Chapter 62

"If you want me again look for me under your boot soles."

Walt Whitman

Gary's inert body rests on the floor—his chest exposed.

Like a puff of steam, another Gary rises from it.

This Gary passes right through the roof and into the night.

Rose and I ascend with him.

We float above the A-frame roof like three shimmering clouds.

Gary's glassy brown eyes are open wide.

Like me, he is barefoot.

Gary is dead.

As thoroughly and irreversibly dead as I am.

As dead as Rose.

Whether he realizes it or not—Gary has become a citizen of the afterlife—with all the responsibilities and privileges thereof.

Gary looks down at the roof, then lifts his gaze—bewildered.

When Gary sees us, his pupils contract in horror. "Who are you?"

"I'm Charles," I say amiably, trying to counteract his revulsion. "Charles Stone. And this is Rose. I am—was—Cali's stepfather. I came here to see if we could help her."

I extend my hand to Gary, but he does not accept it.

Rose lowers her head and wags her tail in greeting, then floats toward Gary.

Gary retreats from Rose.

"What's wrong with you?"

I assume Gary refers to my unfortunate appearance—disheveled, barefoot, with exposed gunshot wounds in my neck, my grayish skin—the whole unsavory death package that is me.

"I was shot to death," I explain—deciding not to sugarcoat the less than optimal the situation in which we find ourselves.

Gary looks me up and down.

Then he stares at Rose. "And what about the dog? Why does she look like that?"

Poor Rose. No amount of post-mortal love from me can fatten her up. She died starving and thirsty and so she remains for eternity.

"When Rose was alive she was mistreated."

Gary looks at his cyanotic fingers. "I'm dreaming, right? This is a nightmare."

"You're not dreaming," I say gently. "You're not even sleeping. You're dead."

Gary nods. "Yeah. I had an asthma attack."

"After that worthless piece of shit sadistic coward had you in a chokehold." I float closer to Gary. "I'm really sorry."

Gary wrings his now-bodiless hands.

"How long have you been dead?" Gary asks after a long moment.

"A couple years," I say. "It's not so bad," I add quickly. "No pain. No suffering."

Gary moves close to Rose. She responds with grateful wags of her tail and a sweet, upturned gaze.

Then Gary surveys the roof of the A-frame below him, the contours of the Dumpsters, the gravel paths assuming clarity in the lessening of darkness that comes before the light of dawn.

"Will I stay with you and the dog?"

"I don't think so," I say. "From what I can tell, each of us occupies our own death—just the way we occupy our own lives—pretty much alone."

Now it's my turn to wonder if I am dreaming.

Gary is fading as a shadow fades when a cloud covers the sun.

He is becoming more and more transparent.
Does he know?

"That's okay." See-through Gary shrugs. "I'm used to being by myself."

"But you never know what will happen," I offer quickly, trying to reassure the poor dead and dissolving kid. "I didn't expect Rose and there she was. It's been good getting to know her."

Gary is almost completely gone now—like the soon-to-break skin of a thinning soap bubble.

"Charles. Get Cali out of here," Gary urges—just a small voice now—"before they kill her, too."

Chapter 63

"We are the dead. Our only true life is in the future. We shall take part in it as handfuls of dust and splinters of bone."

George Orwell

Rose and I remain above the A-frame roof in sombre and respectful silence as the admonition of the newly dead Gary Chung fades into oblivion.

Then I look down.

Rose understands—just as she understands everything worth knowing.

We descend together into the room where Gary died.

Gary's body still rests on the floor. Rose drifts above it and waits.

John sits on his haunches next to the body, his gaze on Nora. Parvati sits on the edge of the small couch, her head tilted. Bennion is still standing, but has moved a few steps closer to the doorway.

"He's dead," John says.

Nora and Parvati exchange a frightened look.

Bennion is calm, but his jaw is working. "The body has to be out of here before daylight," he says. "Undress him. Then bury him and burn his clothes."

Bennion turns, opens the door, and pauses. "And The Seeking will begin this morning. I want the kids out of here. I'll let Rita know."

Chapter 64

"Life is a great sunrise. I do not see why death should not be an even greater one."

Vladamir Nabokov

It is still dark when Parvati and Nora, wearing puffy jackets, jeans, wool caps and boots and headlamps, noisily enter the cabin where Cali and the others are housed.

"Get outside!" Nora commands.

"Move, maggots!" Parvati shouts.

As the young people hurry from their beds, sleep and distrust in their downcast eyes, I look around for Cali. She has complied with Nora's order and she is back in her cot. Rose drifts to her and remains next to her small form.

"You, too, Cali Green," Parvati orders, a dark expression on her face.

Cali quickly follows the others outside the small building.

The kids huddle together for warmth, some in shoes like Cali, some in flip-flops or barefoot.

I notice a cardboard box with "Ramen" printed on the side in a pile of gear and boxes—sleeping bags, small backpacks, small canteens.

The cruel, sad night has faded behind the loaf-shaped mountain's jagged silhouette. Although I can't feel it, I know the inky blue draining from the sky is cold— the way you know the ocean is cold without having to test its coldness with your toes.

Cali moves into the shadows a few feet away from the group. Rose follows her and rests her gaunt on her stomach just above the ground, her sad face on her paws.

Parvati steps quickly to Cali.

"Get back with the group," she hisses.

Rose barks a warning that Parvati doesn't hear.

"Where's Gary?" Cali asks softly. "Is he okay?"

"Gary is fine," Parvati says quickly. "He's on his way back with John from Urgent Care in town. He had an asthma attack, that's all. It looked bad but it wasn't serious."

Cali walks back to where the group is standing.

"Today begins the most important experience you will have at this school," Nora is saying. "Today you will begin The Seeking,"

The kids are wary—waiting to hear what this means.

Parvati removes a small flat drum from a sack on the ground and begins to tap it. The drum looks like something she purchased in a toy shop. It has a crappy white feather attached to its side and a fake animal hide surface.

"The Seeking will bring you face to face with someone you have been running away from. You. And your weakness. " Nora continues, as if by rote. "The Seeking will unmask your lies."

Parvati chimes in, "And all the pain and shame you've caused your families."

Parvati glances pointedly at Cali.

"Look at the mountain," Parvati orders. The kids swivel their heads and look.

I look, too. I can't help it.

It's big.

High and cold. A rock. Blue against a blue-black sky.

That's fucking all. Why the oohing and ahhing over a rock?

The drumbeats come more quickly now.

Parvati speaks. "You will have two days to reach the summit and to return. Two days without lies or excuses-- you will have only yourselves to rely on. You will each have a backpack, a sleeping bag, a canteen filled with water, a metal bowl, three packets of Ramen, and three granola bars."

I know the calories in packaged ramen from all the years I tried to lose weight and failed— 400 calories--5 grams of protein. 7 grams of fat. So two days with one and 1/2 packets of ramen per day and a 150 calorie granola bar adds up to 600 or so calories—that's not enough.

"What happens if we don't make it?" A barefoot boy has raised his hand timidly as if he's in a classroom. Is this the new Gary?

Parvati says, "If you fail, you will be banished from the group. You will sleep outside in the rocks and the dirt."

The boy looks as though he is about to cry, but Parvati keeps at him. "Look around, Eric. There's an endless supply of rocks for you to move. Insects to eat. And the Dumpsters get filled with garbage each day. The way you're going, you'll probably be living outdoors for the next year."

Chapter 65

"I look upon death to be as necessary..."

Benjamin Franklin

By the time the sun burns above Roca Azul, each young person, Cali among them, has received his or her small military green backpack containing the ramen packets and granola bars from Parvati or from Nora.

Aluminum canteens hang from straps on their shoulders. And each has a thin sleeping bag rolled into a tight cylinder under an arm, and carries the thin blanket under which they slept.

Nora removes some car keys from a pocket. Parvati nods at her. "Okay, it's time."

The kids tramp along the path until they're in the front of the small main building.

Rita stands there waiting for them.

The black pickup truck that brought Cali here is parked where it was before. A second truck, a dusty white one, is parked next to it. Nora walks to the back of the black truck and lowers the tailgate.

The kids walk to the truck, then, one by one, climb into the open bed.

Rita shuts the tailgates of both trucks, then watches them drive away.

Chapter 66

"I'd hate to die twice. It's so boring."

Richard Feynman

As the trucks move down the narrow road, Bennion appears from behind the main building and joins Rita.

"I have a job for someone with advanced organizational skills," he says and smiles. "In other words, you."

"What is it? Not the website, I hope." Rita smiles back. "I can't seem to get that new program to work for me."

"No," Bennion says. "I just need you to spend a few hours in my office. My personal filing system has gotten out of hand. And I need you to start printing the address labels for the next mailing of the brochures."

"Sure," Rita says. "I wouldn't mind a morning in town."

Chapter 67

"When death tells a story you really have to listen"

Markus Zusak

Rose's steady gaze doesn't waver from the road on which the truck carrying Cali has traveled.

I watch Rita leave, then Bennion turn and walk around the back of the main building.

What do we do?

Do we go with Cali or follow Bennion?

Cali is probably safe. At least for a little while.

She's with the group and out in the open.

I have to find out why Bennion wants the whole place to himself.

"Rosie," I say, "We'll see Cali soon. Right now, come with me."

Rose takes one last look at the road before she floats with me above Bennion as he trots to the tool shed and removes a bucket and a shovel.

Chapter 68

"There is no death! What seems so is transition;
This life of mortal breath
Is but a suburb..."

Henry Wadsworth Longfellow

Maybe Bennion intends to help John with Gary's burial.

Bennion carries the bucket over his large wrist, and has the shovel over his shoulder as he turns away from the path and climbs the thickly wooded hill.

Bennion doesn't stop at the top, but scrambles down until he reaches the bottom of a rocky ravine.

This place is empty and hidden from view.

John isn't here.

And there is no fresh mound of earth denoting Gary's final resting place.

Bennion puts the bucket down. Then the shovel.

He looks over his shoulder, then takes a stone and silver inlaid knife from his belt and kneels near a large, flat, red rock.

Bennion uses the flat blade of his knife to pry the rock off the ground.

The red earth beneath has been recently disturbed. Bennion brushes the gravel away with his big, tan hands. Then he picks up his shovel and digs.

Chapter 69

"There is a remedy for all things but death…"

Cervantes

Rose and I watch Bennion work.

The soil is gritty and light and looks as though it came from somewhere else.

Finally Bennion kneels by the hole again, and digs by hand.

I'm worried about Cali. This is taking way too long.

Rose seems worried, too. She floats high above the treetops and stares in the direction of Roca Azul.

What is it Bennion's got buried here? Money? Why should I give a shit?

Then I see something.

The curved contours of a pale object under Bennion's hands.

Bennion works frantically now, removing earth until a pottery bowl—face down in the ground—is free.

Time and the earth have stained cracked bowl the color of strong tea.

A hole has been drilled in the center. And a piece is missing—about the size of the shard Bennion showed Rebecca in the gallery.

Rose, who has been floating in aimless circles above Bennion, suddenly becomes interested in the bowl.

Ears back, she darts down to the hole in the center and begins to bark.

Chapter 70

"O praise and praise
For the sure-enwinding arms of cool-enfolding Death."

Walt Whitman

Bennion gingerly carefully places the bowl on the ground.

Rose's barks become more insistent.

She wants to return to Cali, I'm sure.

But in a few minutes I'll know what Bennion is hiding here.

"Wait," I tell Rose. "Please, Rosie. Wait."

Below the bowl is another is bowl-shaped object.

Bennion works quickly to liberate it from the earth.

What the fuck?

It's the coffee-colored dome of a human skull.

This is Bennion's "special project"?

Bennion roughly separates the skull from the skeleton, and tosses it aside. Then he resumes his methodical excavation.

I look closely at the skull. It's too old to belong to a kid.

I'm going to find out whose head this is.

"Rose," I say, "Come."

Rose follows me as we descend into the ground, down below the skeleton's headless shoulders—then below the long bones of its feet—until we're at the bottom of a deep pit.

The skeleton sits in the fetal position above us. Pottery—some decorated with brown paint and shaped like animals—shells, bits of turquoise and parts of other objects dot the earth.

I know enough to recognize this place as a Native American grave. And to see that that the man or woman buried here was lovingly placed, the objects carefully arranged around him or her.

Rose whines—and sinks a little farther down.

I follow her until she stops at a yellowish thing deep below the skeleton.

A blanket?

No.

Jesus.

It's a mummified dog, its body folded tightly on its side, its face—eyes closed—its head still resting on its paws.

Chapter 71

"Is death a door that leads to light?"

Robert Green Ingersoll

When Rose and I ascend from the burial pit and return to Bennion, he's yanking the skeleton apart in order to reach the pottery below it.

A dog growls.

This growl is meaner and deeper than Rose's.

Where is it coming from?

Rose whines in answer, then sails toward the bowl that covered the skull.

As I follow Rose the canine voice gets louder as I approach the bowl.

Then I remember Bennion's conversation with Rebecca.

Can this hole be what Rebecca called "the kill hole"?

Does it mean that the person buried here was murdered?

Rose barks in excitement.

A blur—sort of like smoke—emerges from the hole. Then the blur intensifies and contracts until it is a dog with yellow fur and bared teeth.

A dark stone arrowhead protrudes from its side.

An old man—copper-skinned and naked—appears next from the opening in the bowl. He has a large gash in his leg—the wound runs from hip to knee, the blood coagulated and black.

Rose whines and her tail swings back and forth.

Jesus.

This must be the dead Indian from the pit.

And his dead dog.

And they both look really, really pissed.

Chapter 72

"There are worse things waiting for men than death."

Algernon Charles Swinburne

The dead man and the dog glide close to Bennion as he gingerly removes a decorated, narrow-necked jar from the pit.

The dead man angrily shouts words that are heavy on sh and hard t sounds—at Bennion that he does not hear and which I do not understand. Then the man purses his brown, withered lips and releases a long, high-pitched whistle.

Rose cocks her ears as the eerie whistle hangs in the silence and then dies.

The Indian frowns at me, drifts back to the bowl, and disappears into the hole.

But yellow dog approaches Rose and growls.

Rose averts her eyes submissively and flattens her ears.

Then she sits midair—her tail tucked under her haunches—her mouth in an odd grin.

The yellow dog studies Rose's strange expression and relaxes.

Rose whines.

The yellow dog barks three times, then turns away from Rose and sinks into the darkness of the small opening in the bowl.

Rose floats to the bowl, sniffs the hole and looks at me pleadingly.

"No," I say to Rose. "No."

I feel sorry for the man whose peaceful death Bennion has so callously disturbed. Ditto for the poor, mummified dog and for whatever the fuck happened to it.

I'm sorry Bennion has looted what must be their sacred resting place.

But this man's death is his own business.

The dog and the stuff in his grave are his problem.

I'm here for Cali.

"Let's go find Cali," I say. "Come on, Rosie. Let's go."

Rose's eyes widen when she hears Cali's name, but something much more potent pulls her gaze away from me.

"Rosie!" I call sharply as—like water traveling down a drain—Rose vanishes into the deep darkness beyond the opening in the ancient bowl.

Chapter 73

"Neither the sun nor death can be looked at with a steady eye."

La Rochefoucauld

Death is more cruel, more complicated—more opaque and baffling—than I could ever know.

I understand that Rose was never mine—I am hers.

The feeling that I ever "had" her—or could relinquish her—is a selfish delusion.

Rose has her own truth.

She acts according to her own, pure will.

Did she follow the dead Indian and the dog God knows where out of curiosity?

Or is going with them something Rose is meant to do?

The barren solitude in which I find myself does not provide answers—or even clues.

Does Rose expect me to wait for her?

To hang around as Bennion packs up his stolen pottery and fills in the grave with bones and dirt?

Well I can't fucking do that.

I can't abandon Cali again.

Even if it means that I'll lose Rose.

Chapter 74

"The long mysterious exodus of death..."

Henry Wadsworth Longfellow

The trucks move toward Roca Azul on a narrow curving road. Cali and the others sit quietly, some with eyes closed, others staring out at the grassy plateau and the forested ridges above it.

After about twenty minutes, Parvati, and Nora turn the pickups into a paved parking lot enclosed by tall pines. A brown and beige wooden sign says, "Roca Azul Wilderness Trail."

The lot is empty.

Parvati exits her truck first, then Nora, and lowers the tailgates.

"Get out, maggots," Parvati orders. The kids look around and climb out of the trucks. Ribbons of wind make the dark, tall trees' branches wobble.

"Follow me, maggots," Parvati instructs as she walks purposefully across the empty lot and to the place where the paving ends and a small dirt path begins. The young people follow her and stop when she stops, maybe thirty feet past the trees.

This is not what I expected after all their threats.

I rise in the air and see that the narrow footpath meanders across the plateau, ascending gently until it disappears behind the tree-line. After that it moves far up along Roca Azul's lapis lazuli spine to the top.

There's even a pond visible far off in the flat grassy space. It gleams like a piece of wet blue slate in the light of dawn.

This place is beautiful.

I look at the expanse of dry yellow grass and imagine Rose skimming its undulating surface like a bird.

But now Rose has become a ghost of a ghost—and I am diminished because she is no longer with me.

The kids march single file with Parvati in the lead. Nora walks at the end, establishing the pace with beats on the fake drum. I begin to hear birds—don't ask me what kind—loud tweeting and singing. For all I know the birds are arguing or complaining. Screaming maybe. Threatening their young. Calling each other ugly names.

Bennion's probably in the gallery back room by now, showing off his loot to Rebecca, who's dialing the phone numbers of her rich Parisian collectors.

Cali appears safe.

For now.

I must find out where they put Gary's body.

Chapter 75

The empty school is as silent as a premonition.

As I drift above the path up the hill, I hear dull thuds coming from the clearing where the kids moved the stones for Bennion's parking lot.

When I reach the clearing I see Gary's naked body.

He rests on a blue painter's tarp, his blank eyes staring skyward and his mouth stiffened into an angry grimace.

John—shirtless—excavates a small, deep grave.

When John is satisfied the hole is deep enough, he puts the shovel down, gives Gary's body a long look, then wraps the tarp tightly around it and pushes it into the hole.

John quickly covers Gary's body with earth, then tamps the surface flat with the soles of his work shoes.

John does a good job. Except for a slight difference in the fresh dirt's color—it's almost impossible tell the surface was ever disturbed.

But isn't it stupid to bury the body here, right at the school?

Maybe not.

Who would dream that Bennion could have the nerve to plant Gary's body right below his brand new state of the art parking lot?

Chapter 76

Death …is a stopped watch, a loss, an end, a darkness. Nothing."

Ray Bradbury

John angles the shovel over his shoulder and trots down past the Dumpsters to the A-frame where Gary died, dropping the shovel on the ground outside.

John enters the A-Frame and walks to the small kitchen. He turns on the tap and scrubs the dust and dirt from his face, hands and arms with dish soap and water.

He dries his face with a dishtowel, takes out his cell phone, and punches a number into the keypad.

The phone is on speaker.

"Is it done?" asks Bennion's voice.

"Yes," John says. "We should expedite the surfacing of the parking lot."

"Fine. And his clothes?"

"Not yet," John says.

"In a few hours I'm going to have to announce that Gary Chung is a runaway. You have to dispose of his clothing right now."

There is a click as Bennion ends the call.

John opens the cupboard below the kitchen sink and takes out a black trash bag. Then he enters the living area. Gary's clothes are still on the floor. John picks them up and stuffs them into the bag.

Chapter 77

"Do not seek death. Death will find you."

Dag Hammarskjöld

John drives a gray Ford Focus on the same road Nora and Parvati followed in the trucks. The black plastic garbage bag with Gary's empty clothing inside it occupies the space next to him in the passenger seat.

John passes the parking lot where Nora and Parvati parked, and drives a few more minutes before turning onto a dirt road blocked by a padlocked metal gate.

John kills the engine, takes a bolt-cutter from the trunk, cuts open the padlock, and shoulders the gate open.

He drives through, then gets out of the car and closes the gate.

The road—which might be an old logging road—narrows on its curving ascent. John drives what must be halfway to the top and stops near a stand of trees, their branches thrashing in the wind.

John grabs the trash bag and gets out of the car, then opens the trunk again.

Inside—way in the back—is a can of gasoline.

John takes the gas can in one hand and the trash bag in the other. He hikes for about fifteen minutes until he reaches a small clearing.

John places the bag on the ground and kneels, gathering dry sticks and leaves with his hands, and piling them on the bag.

Then John opens the nozzle, and pours gasoline over the plastic bag.

He lights a match, drops the matchbook on the bag, and quickly steps back a few paces.

Flames—yellow-orange and white—jump from the bag with a huge "whomp" sound.

The bag writhes and crackles as the fire consumes it.

When the flames rise as high as John's shoulders, he retreats through the trees toward his car.

A strong gust of wind sends sparks and swirling bits of burning plastic into the branches of the trees.

A low branch, and then another glow and begin to burn.

Chapter 78

> *"...They perished in the seamless grass,*
> *No eye could find the place..."*

Emily Dickinson

What if the fire moves toward the mountain? John won't—can't—call the fire department, can he?

He'll have to let the hillside—and the mountain if the fire grows--burn.

Cali and kids have to get out right now.

But when I arrive at the path, I'm relieved to see that the kids have made surprisingly little progress.

The mountain still seems very far away.

How long will they walk like this, trudging toward a fire they can't see?

Nora and Parvati urge them forward when they lag.

I stay a few inches above Cali, scanning the mountain for smoke.

And I can't prevent myself for looking for Rose's graceful slender shape floating toward me above the trees.

No smoke is visible yet.

No Rose.

A girl asks if she can stop to pee. Parvati says no. Nora keeps beating the drum, setting the pace at which the group must walk.

Finally they reach a narrowing in the path. Parvati stops walking and Nora refrains from beating the drum.

The wind picks up. Rough gusts carrying dust and bits of brittle grass into the air.

"Because you are maggots, you should climb the rest of the way on your filthy bellies," Parvati says and glances toward the mountain. "But that would take too long."

Nora looks grim.

"No. All you have to do is hike. Up to the mountain and then back down again. Now that shouldn't be too tough. Even for stupid shit-eating maggots like you."

Nora inspects the scraggly line of kids, then, stops at Eric, the slowest in the group, the last one in the line. "Except for you, Eric." Nora says. "Lie down."

Eric pales, then drops to his knees and lies face down on the path. The backpack he wears on his shoulder slides up over the back of his head. The canteen sits uncomfortably under his hip.

"Crawl, maggot," Nora orders.

A sob ripples through his skinny body like a wave. Eric doesn't move.

Nora kicks him in the ribs. "You heard me, maggot. Crawl."

Chapter 79

Eric struggles on all fours along the path.

"Move!" Parvati yells at the back of Eric's head. "Do you hear me? Move!"

Eric stops. He's finished.

Nora kicks Eric again. He groans, but stays where he is.

Parvati unscrews the top to a water bottle and pours the contents on Eric's head.

"Maggots," Parvati says, "Come here. Now. Eric seems to need some motivation."

The kids walk slowly toward Eric.

"Closer," Nora orders and they shuffle closer, and she kicks Eric's thigh. "Now it's your turn," she says and looks at the girl with brown hair.

"I can't," the girl says.

"Yes you can," Nora says, "unless you want to crawl, too."

The girl looks at the ground and then kicks Eric's side, the dirty flip-flop on her foot flapping against his shoulder.

"You call that a kick?" Parvati says. "Next."

One by one the kids kick Eric. Few wear serious shoes, so the blows are more symbolic than damaging. Eric keeps his face pressed in the dirt to muffle his sobs.

Now it is Cali's turn.

She stands with her arms crossed against her chest. She does not move.

"Green. Cali Green," Parvati says, "Come here."

"No." Cali says.

"No?" Parvati asks, her face flushing with anger. "Did I hear you say 'no'?"

"Leave him alone," Cali says. "Just leave him alone, okay?"

"She ordered you to help Eric become motivated," Nora says. "Now do as you're told."

"No." Cali straightens up and says. "I won't."

Chapter 80

Death hath so many doors to let out life.

Beaumont and Fletcher

Cali relinquishes her bedroll, canteen and backpack to the dry grass and takes off —still clutching her blanket— toward the tree line.

The winds have turned the grassy plateau into a choppy sea.

As Cali sprints across, she is like a lone swimmer fighting the open sea.

Will Nora or Parvati go after her? And if they reach Cali, what will they do?

Nora scowls in anger, then squints at the trees.

"Don't bother," Parvati says. "There's nowhere she can go but up. Otherwise we'll see her. And we'll find her anyhow. Just wait. "

Parvati nods at the backpack on the ground. "She'll be crawling back towards the parking lot in an hour or two, begging for water and food."

Chapter 81

"Think not disdainfully of death, but look on it with favour..."

Marcus Aurelius Antoninus

Cali approaches trees—and I float right above her—more permeable than a moonbeam, lighter than a filament in a spider's web, more slippery than thought—you know the goddamn drill.

But Cali is substantial.

Mortal.

Combustible.

As I reach the tree-line, I look back at the line of kids shuffling behind Eric as he painfully crawls along once again.

If hikers saw them, what would they think of Bennion's "wilderness therapy"? What would Nora or Parvati say to explain Eric's misery?

The living only see and hear what they want to see and hear.

Cali reaches the shadowed place below the trees and keeps going, pushing through decaying branches and climbing over gray-blue rocks.

Her eyes are wild. Her uneven short hair seems to stand on end. She looks deranged. If Nora or Parvati wanted to, they could probably get her committed.

But they won't.

Although she doesn't realize it now, Cali witnessed Gary's murder.

They have to keep her around---until they can get rid of her.

Chapter 82

"What we call life is a journey to death. What we call death is the gateway to life."

Wayne Triplett

Cali fights her way through the rough terrain, stopping finally to catch her breath below a rocky ledge.

I move so close to Cali that my bloodless hands disappear into her shoulders as I try to shake them.

"Don't stop!" I shout. "There's a fire. And Gary's dead. John killed him!"

But all Cali hears is the wind, and carried within it, small high-pitched sounds coming somewhere beyond or behind the ledge.

I ascend above Cali to take a look. There's a small opening among a jumble of flat rocks.

Inside the dark opening a small canine nose and two black eyes are visible. Then another pair and another.

Three small canine shapes with soft, grayish fur. They whine again and turn their heads back toward the opening.

Instead of moving on, Cali looks up at the ledge, searching for the source of the sound.

The air is smoky and the wind is picking up.

Shit.

I need to find a way to get her out of here.

Without thinking and before I can stop myself, I turn toward the fire and the darkening air—and I call for Rose.

Chapter 83

"Death rides on every passing breeze,
He lurks in every flower."

Reginald Heber

"Rosie!"

But Rose does not arrive in answer to my call.

Why did I think she would?

Can she hear me? Or is she ignoring my voice?

The pups have moved from the opening and whimper in fear.

Cali sees them now, and stares at them, intent and worried.

Are they coyotes?

Wolves?

Wolves live in packs, don't they? If they're wolves, then others may be close.

Big ones.

Chapter 84

"Life'll kill ya…"

Warren Zevon

White flecks of ash and sparks whirl angrily in the smoky air, but Cali stays where she is below the ledge.

How close is the fire?

I rise through the thrashing branches until I'm above the treetops.

A pillar of orange smoke approaches, alive with sparks. Strong bursts of wind are braiding and untangling it, as it elongates and widens.

Seeds of fire flash and begin to bloom below me in the trees.

Fuck.

The cubs whine on the ledge.

Why don't they run away?

I pass through the small opening in the rocks and enter a small, dark den. In the back a large canine form rests on its side.

Its amber eyes are open and glassy and its fur is stained wine-red.

I move near it and see that the front legs are stiff.

This animal is dead.

A trap—lead chain still attached—has almost severed one of its bloody back legs.

Chapter 85

"Come lovely and soothing death,
Undulate round the world, serenely arriving, arriving . . . "

Walt Whitman

When I move out of the den, Cali is tightening her blanket around her hips. But instead of running away from the fire, she starts climbing the jagged rocks, up toward the ledge.

What the hell is she thinking?

She scrambles up over the rocks, losing her shoes, her socks ripping and exposing the soles of her feet as she goes.

Cali makes it just below the ledge and stops. She looks up, then stands on bare tiptoes on the edge of a curved outcropping, and reaches with her fingertips for the edge.

Above her the fire's flames dance from branch to branch.

The pups growl as Cali tries to hoist herself up and onto the ledge.

Then in what seems like slow motion, Cali loses her footing and falls.

Cali's body meets the rocky ground with a dull sound, and then she is still.

Cali's eyes are closed, but I see no blood, just a beet-colored bruise on her forehead, a gash on her chin, and scrapes on her arms and legs.

Chapter 86

"Death borders upon our birth, and our cradle stands in the grave."

Joseph Hall

Voiceless and bodiless—how can I rouse Cali?

How can I save the orphaned cubs?

You know what my options are right now?

I can haul my fat ass back to the kingdom of death.

Or I can watch Cali and the wolf cubs burn.

Again, I summon Rose.

"Rose," I shout. "Cali needs our help!"

Nothing.

Then I remember the Indian.

Chapter 87

"Fear death?
... No! let me taste the whole of it ..."

Robert Browning

I look at Cali unconscious on the ground.

At the stranded cubs whining and yipping on the ledge.

The volatile air thickens and turns orange.

The only chance I have of saving them is to leave them.

But before go I say what I should have said—and felt—long ago when I was alive and she could hear me—

Cali.

I love you.

Chapter 88

"Time flies, death urges..."

Edward Young

Returning to the Indian art gallery was a mistake.

I should have known that Bennion would never trust such a valuable object to anyone except himself.

So I am in his unoccupied office—hoping it isn't already too late.

The lights are off and the blinds are closed. A string of red chili pepper lights on the wall of the small reception area provides the only illumination.

Nothing here except a fresh pile of Serene Mountain brochures and a flat of bottled mummified in heavy plastic wrap.

I melt through the wall and into the back office.

Bennion's computer is on.

The screen saver—a color photograph of a dog howling open-mouthed at the moon from the top of Roca Azul—lights the way to Bennion's cluttered desk.

Reports. Files. More brochures. Coffee cup. A paper plate covered with crumbs.

I dart around the small space like a frightened goldfish—quickly scanning every surface.

Nothing.

I return to the desk and notice see a pair Bennion's ornate cowboy boots pushed way in the back underneath.

I enter the left boot.

A thick sock has collapsed inside the pointed toe.

I find the sock's mate in the other boot—but there's something else—the bowl Bennion looted from the Indian's grave is wedged in sideways like a half-moon.

But it's not the bowl I want—I'm here for the small opening drilled into its base.

Will I be able to undo what I'm about to do?

Fucking coward that I am—I close my eyes——and dive into the kill hole's murky gloom.

Chapter 89

We are all of us resigned to death: it's life we aren't resigned to."

Graham Greene

I open my eyes to a dead and silent world.

A vast plateau—drained of color—reaches for a black not-sky.

The silence is so absolute, I wonder if I have become deaf.

Will I be able to find my way back to Cali in time?

Or is she—and like Rose—forever lost to me?

"Rose!" I shout.

But the emptiness devours the sound.

I float toward the horizon—involuntarily scanning for Rose's delicate-as-a-shadow, slender silhouette—until I reach nothing and then the nothing after that.

If the dead Indian, the yellow dog and Rose came here through the kill hole—then where the hell did they go?

Chapter 90

"Death hath so many doors to let out life."

Beaumont and Fletcher

I give the fuck up.

I am adrift and becoming more lost as I float through—or does it float through me? —the featureless, surfaceless, colorless, substance-less post mortal fog—though I say fog just to give you, who are alive in the ROYGIV, textured, solid world—a vague idea of what this place is.

My plan to save Cali—and to find Rose—was a joke.

On them.

On me.

For all I goddamn know, I'm stuck here for eternity—alone.

Chapter 91

"The last to be overcome is death, and the knowledge of life is the knowledge of death."

Edgar Cayce

How long have I been here?

A few seconds?

A thousand years?

I understand what Milton meant when he said hell had "no light, but rather darkness visible."

There's no light here. No here here. No up, no down, no in, no out. No time.

Or is there?

Below my gray bare feet—the nothingness contracts into a small, dark place.

I drift down and see a small black opening—about the size of the opening in Bennion's bowl.

Chapter 92

"A man is not completely born until he is dead."

Benjamin Franklin

I look down—but don't see the kill hole in Bennion's stolen bowl.

I rise like smoke from a hole in the earthen floor of a circular, stone room.

A fire pit has been dug in the center.

Three white flame-like shapes shimmer above the pit.

The dead Indian.

The mummified yellow dog.

And Rose.

Chapter 93

"It's funny the way most people love the dead. Once you're dead, you're made for life."

Jimi Hendrix

"Rosie!" I call. "Rose!"

Rose flies from the mummified dog's wounded side to me.

The dead Indian and the mummified yellow dog watch impassively as Rose descends, pushes her bony head against my chin, then joyfully licks my face with her dry tongue.

"We have to help Cali," I say to Rose. "Now."

Rose's eyes widen.

She turns toward the Indian and his yellow dog and howls, then produces a series of sharp, short barks.

The yellow dog stiffens and repeats Rose's howls and barks.

The dead Indian's black eyes darken.

He shouts something I do not understand, and then whistles.

Chapter 94

"Death is like a mirror in which the true meaning of life is reflected."

Sogyal Rinpoche

The flames—carried here on the wind—close in and ignite the trees above the rocky ledge.

Above Cali.

But inside the wind's roar a long, shrill whistle is audible.

Rose whines in answer as she hovers next to me.

Yes.

As the dead Indian and the yellow dog appear among the flames, I hear the Indian's whistle once again.

Chapter 95

"Of all the gods, Death only craves not gifts:
Nor sacrifice, nor yet drink-offering poured
Avails; no altars hath he, nor is soothed
By hymns of praise."

Aeschylus

Rustling.

Then deep barks and snorts.

Five living wolves appear from the shadows and rush toward Cali.

The small ones hang back a few paces.

But the big ones move frighteningly close to Cali's unmoving form.

Their yellow eyes smolder.

Their wet teeth are visible in their open mouths as faces move close to hers.

I silently beg Cali to remain unconscious, as the leanest, largest wolf roughly paws Cali's face and neck.

I implore the fire to come close enough to scare them off.

The smaller ones in the back rush forward now, growling, nipping at Cali's hands and legs.

Chapter 96

"I would fain die a dry death."

Shakespeare, The Tempest

The wolf snorts and paws Cali's face again.

Cali moves her head, her eyes still closed.

Rose hovers right above the living wolf.

Quiet. Tense.

The Indian hocwea near the ledge.

But the mummified dog drifts down to Rose and barks sharply.

The largest wolf blinks and drags its claws across Cali's injured forehead, her cheeks and her eyelids, leaving scratches bright with fresh blood.

Cali moans, reaches for her face, and opens her eyes.

Chapter 97

"Your body is a lock. Death is the key. The key turns... and you're free."

Joe Hill

When Cali sees the wolf's amber, glowing eyes, she screams.

The dead Indian makes a clicking sound, and the yellow dog meekly returns to him.

The Indian whistles again and the wolves retreat— disappearing through the trees and away from the fire.

Sparks whirl.

The pups whine from the ledge.

Rose gives me a look and floats away from Cali and toward the yellow dog.

Then, floating shoulder to shoulder, Rose and the yellow dog hover over the stranded cubs and look at me.

Cali gingerly touches her face and then looks up intently at the ledge.

Chapter 98

*"Who knows but life be that which men call death
And death what men call life?"*

Euripides

Cali stands shakily, then touches the blanket tied around her hips.

She looks up at the cubs.

Then, from a different starting point, she begins the climb to the ledge again.

This time Cali navigates twenty vertical feet and is able to pull herself onto the surface of the ledge.

On the ledge, the pups tremble and whine, pawing at the opening among the rocks.

"What is it?" Cali says. She flattens herself and peers inside.

Chapter 99

"It is not the whole of life to live,
Nor all of death to die."

James Montgomery

Cali squints and sees the dead wolf inside. "Oh no. You poor thing."

Rose and the yellow dog watch intently as Cali unties the blanket and places it on the ledge, then quickly scoops the cubs onto the blanket.

The dead Indian watches her from above—where he floats among smouldering branches— then his dead eyes meet mine.

He nods.

I nod back.

Cali ties the ends of the blanket together, securing the animals inside. The cubs are quiet as Cali slips the blanket over her neck and begins the descent.

When I look up, the mummified dog and the Indian are gone.

Chapter 100

"By daily dying, I have come to be."

Theodore Roethke

Cali—with the wolf cubs secured in the blanket—runs away from the fire.

Away from Roca Azul.

As Rose and I float above her, we hear the rush of wings and skittering sounds as other animals flee the flames.

Rose stays close to me—very close.

After about thirty minutes, Cali emerges from the trees onto the plateau.

Smoke masks the mountain and the sky. Behind her silhouette the fire is a shimmer of light inside the trees.

As we drift behind Cali, I wonder how flammable the dry plateau is, if Cali has the strength to cross it, and what will be waiting for her if she succeeds.

Chapter 101

"Death can be kind."

Catherynne M. Valente

Lights and voices fill the pewter air as Cali limps to the edge of the parking lot where Parvati and Nora parked—it seems like years ago.

A park ranger's off-road vehicle, an ambulance, and two yellow fire trucks are parked there at odd angles—lights flashing red and blue.

There is no sign of Parvati or Nora, the kids or the trucks.

Cali glances back at something in the grass, then moves toward the ranger's truck.

A female ranger in hiking boots and a wide-brimmed hat sees Cali, and trots toward her, speaking into a walkie-talkie as she goes.

"Are you hurt?" She asks? "Are you alone?"

"I was with a group from Serene Mountain School," Cali says. "But I don't know where they are now."

"Don't worry," the ranger says." "They're safe. What happened to you, Miss?"

"I fell, but I'm okay," Cali says. "But there are some animals back there—"Cali looks back toward the high grass——they breathed in a lot of smoke."

"Okay," the ranger says, and waves toward the off-road vehicle. A male ranger gets out and she shouts, "We need a large kennel and the collar."

The man retrieves a large plastic carrier and carries a pole with a snare collar at one end—the kind dog catchers use.

Cali leads the rangers to the grass and unties the blanket. The pups blink and cower.

The rangers exchange a look.

"Do you know what that they are, Miss?" the male ranger asks.

"Coyotes?" Cali says.

"Wolves. Mexican gray wolves. They're endangered. But we can't seem to stop hunters from shooting and trapping them—they sell the fur. Let's get you looked at and load these animals into the truck."

The ranger wraps up the pups in the blanket, places them inside the carrier, and secures the latch.

"I saw their mother. I think a trap killed her. They didn't want to leave her. Even in the fire.

Chapter 102

"Believe me, when you die, it's everybody else's but your problem . . ."

Ceclia Adhern

Roca Azul glows an angry crimson.

An EMT dressed in a dark blue uniform examines Cali inside the ambulance.

Cali is gaunt, bruised, and filthy. Lacerations crisscross her face, neck, feet and arms. The bruise on her forehead has swollen into an angry red bulge. The bloody scratches on her face have coagulated.

"We're going to take you to the hospital in Taos, Miss." The EMT shines a small light into Cali's eyes. "You look dehydrated and like you might have a concussion. When was the last time you drank any water?"

Cali shrugs. "Yesterday maybe. I'm not sure."

"I'm going to start an I.V. to give you some fluids. You'll feel a pinch."

Rose floats a few inches above Cali's chest as a second EMT, a woman, secures her on a gurney and the first EMT inserts the IV needle into Cali's arm.

Chapter 103

In the E.R., Cali is mute as her feet are washed with disinfectant and bandaged, her forehead bruise and facial scratches are cleaned, and when she receives a tetanus shot and antibiotics.

She's still quiet in a small private room where a middle-aged nurse wearing flowered purple scrubs helps her into a gown and then into a hospital bed.

I suspect Cali is afraid—waiting to see who arrives here first—Bennion, her parents or the police.

"Sounds like you had a tough time out there near Roca Azul," a nurse says kindly.

Cali nods, closes her eyes and sleeps.

Rose has made herself small in the air above at the foot of the hspital bed. I float near the monitor and the I.V. pole when the slim shape that is Elaine pauses, then rushes to the hospital bed and embraces Cali. "Oh my God! Elaine says, "What happened? What did they do?"

Cali begins to cry.

Steve enters the hospital room now carrying a small suitcase. He moves behind Elaine and stands near Elaine next to Cali's bed.

Cali finally catches her breath and tears shine on her cheeks. "Don't make me go back there," she pleads. "Please. Steve. Don't make me go back."

Elaine is dressed in plain black pants and a simple black sweater--sort of like running clothes. She's wearing sneakers and her hair is pulled back in a ponytail.

Jesus.
She must have been scared shitless when they left.

Steve speaks. "You're not going back, Cali. I've spoken to Mr. Christian. He's filing an emergency petition with the court right now."

Elaine sits on the bed next to Cali, her manicured hands folded in her lap. For once she shuts the fuck up.

Rose warily studies Elaine's and Steve's every move.

"It's not a school," Cali says. "They fed us garbage. And made us move rocks around all day. The man who runs it? He hit me. And they choked a kid until he passed out."

Elaine begins to cry. "I'm so sorry, Cali. We had no idea."

"Please forgive me," Steve says. "I believed what Christian told me. And the brochure."

Cali says nothing about forgiveness, but looks at Steve intently. "I need you to do something--"

But it is Elaine who speaks first. "Anything," she says, "What is it? What do you need?"

"Tell the police to get the other kids out of there right away."

Elaine nods. But Cali isn't finished. "And call police in LA and drop the charges against Gloria. You know she never stole that purse."

Chapter 104

"I do not think we were afraid of death; life had become such an infinitely boring alternation between a period of stimulation which failed to stimulate and of depression which hardly even depressed."

Aleister Crowley

Rose and I remain with Cali in her hospital room for the next two days.

Rose stays above Cali's chest or at the bed's foot —I'm usually floating halfway up the wall above her head.

Steve booked a room at the Inn at Roca Azul, but Elaine doesn't use it. Although Cali barely speaks to her, she sits in a green plastic chair by the bed or stands looking out the window at the plateau and beyond, at the glowing fire that slowly dies at the mountain's base.

Steve arrives with cardboard cups of hot chocolate, coffee and paper bags of take-out food. He spends most of his time in the hallway talking on his cell phone, his expression grim or angry.

Cali sleeps for hours at a stretch, then wakes to eat the food the nurse brings in on a tray or that Steve brings in Styrofoam containers—scrambled eggs and country fries, grilled cheese sandwiches, sopapillas and little packets of honey, blue corn enchiladas.

Elaine eats too. I've never seen her eat as much or as often and suspect that seeing Cali so thin has something to do with her suddenly-robust appetite.

Late yesterday two uniformed police officers—a man and a woman—entered the room. The man had glossy black hair and a black moustache. The name on his badge was Roblar. The woman was a tall and muscular ash blond. Her badge said Gidding.

They talked to Cali for a long time, Gidding asked questions and Roblar took notes. A few times Elaine interrupted Cali to ask something or to explain—but Roblar would always silence her with a stern look.

Cali told them about the night before the march to Roca Azul. Bennion hitting her. John choking Gary and then carrying him away.

"And did you see Gary after that?" Gidding asked.

"No," Cali says. "But they said John took him to Urgent Care because he had passed out."

"So Gary wasn't with the others on the hike?"

"No. We left before he came back."

Then Cali described Nora and Parvati forcing Eric to crawl. How she ran away and she fell. The fire.

The dead wolf.

The cubs.

But she did not mention the wolves pawing her face. She kept that part of the story to herself.

Patiently and deliberately Officer Gidding always led Cali back to the night that Gary died. Bennion striking her. John choking Gary. Gary's limp body.

Elaine listened—her red eyes filling with tears or her face in her hands.

Steve looked sick. He gnawed his cheek and clenched and unclenched his fists.

Finally Officer Gidding thanked Cali for her cooperation. "Thank you very much, Miss Green," she said. "The information you shared is very helpful."

"What about the others?" Cali asked. "What about Eric?"

"Eric and all but one of the students are accounted for. They're with Child Protective Services," Officer Gidding explained. "Their parents and guardians are on their way."

"All but one?"

"I'm afraid one student is still missing, Miss Green," Officer Gidding said. "A runaway. We have not been able to locate Gary Chung."

Chapter 105

"Death is the possibility of change."

Peter Steinhart

Cali is being discharged from Espíritu Santo Hospital. She wears clean new clothes—black leggings and a sweatshirt that says "I <3 Taos" Steve bought in the hotel gift shop. The bruise and scratches on her forehead have darkened to a sedate purple. Bandages cover her feet.

Elaine pushes the wheelchair. I don't say this gleefully—but she looks awful—her hair is dull and flat and she seems to have forgotten how to apply makeup to her puffy face. Steve schleps Elaine's large handbag and the plastic bag that says "Patient's Belongings." A nurse walks ahead, then opens the lobby doors and leads them into the white light of day.

There is a long covered walkway and then a limo driver and a shiny black Town Car. The driver takes the patient belonging bag from Steve and opens the door. The nurse hugs Cali and then rolls the empty wheelchair toward the lobby.

Cali gets into the car first. It can't help but remind her of Kirby and Witt, but she doesn't hesitate. Elaine follows and then Steve gets in.

Elaine closes her eyes. Steve stares at his BlackBerry. Cali presses her face to the window and studies the landscape.

Smoke encircles Roca Azul like a delicate scarf.

"The news says that the fire is almost contained," the driver finally says to break the silence. "They're not sure what started it. But we often get lightning fires up here."

"I'm glad it's almost out," Cali says. "All the animals that live out there. I hope they could escape."

"You're one of those kids from that wilderness school, aren't you?" the driver asks, looking at Cali's injured face in his rearview mirror.

"Yeah," Cali says.

"Wow. You're lucky to be alive. It's good thing you didn't end up like that kid."

"What kid?" Cali asks.

"The boy who died. Search dogs found his body buried in a dirt lot up at the school."

Chapter 106

"But really death seems the least awful thing that can happen to someone."

Sebastian Horsley

A numb silence surrounds Cali during the plane ride and while another Town Car—this one from LAX—delivers her with Elaine and Steve to the presumptuous and oversized driveway that leads to the giant front door of Elaine's residence.

A maid I've never seen before waits at the top of the curving driveway. She wears the same pink uniform that Gloria did, except that she's younger and much thinner. It's only now that I realize that Elaine must have picked this color to match the kitchen curtains.

Steve emerges from the car first, then Elaine.

The maid stares at Elaine's disheveled hair, the cracked nail polish on her fingers, the freckled skin unmasked by makeup.

Cali slides out and looks around as if what she sees is not completely real. She stays close to the car, her hand on the door's handle. Rose hovers near her shoulders.

The maid winces when she sees how thin Cali is—sees her bruised and lacerated face and bandaged feet.

Elaine and Steve walk toward the entrance of the house, but Cali remains where she is.

"Elaine. Steve," Cali says. "I've thought about it all the way back to L.A. I can't stay here. I just can't live with you guys right now."

Elaine stops, turns and stares at Cali. Steve stops and turns, too.

"What do you mean?" Elaine says. "This is your home."

"I can't. I can't go back inside this house," Cali says quietly. "And I can't go back to my school, either."

Cali looks at Steve. "I've thought about it a lot. I'd like to stay with Gloria awhile. I'm sure she'll let me. Until I figure stuff out, and get my own apartment and maybe a roommate. And Gloria's place is close to the Zoo Magnet High School."

Steve looks at Elaine and shrugs.

Elaine's mouth opens into an O. "You mean you want to live in Van Nuys? Instead of here?" Elaine waves her hand to indicate the house, the grounds—the Tiffany & Co. blue sky above all of it.

"Yes," Cali says. "Yes."

"How can we trust you not to run away again?" Steve asks.

"You can check on me whenever you want. But I won't. I promise," Cali says. "I'm done running away. I mean it."

Chapter 107

"All say, How hard it is we have to die,--a strange complaint to come from the mouths of people who have had to live."

Mark Twain

I learned a few things from our recent expedition into the living world:

The kingdom of the dead is sort of like New Mexico—
Lots of empty space.
Quiet.
Ample opportunities for solitude.
Contemplation.
Revulsion.

A pack of gray wolves attacked Bennion—he was maimed, but he survived.

They say the fire drove the wolves down from the high country and to the Serene Mountain property where they were searching for water.

I think the wolves were looking for something else.

Bennion was charged for the abuses at the school, and for looting an Anasazi grave—a Federal crime.

Rebecca got busted, too—for dealing in stolen antiquities.

That fancy lawyer Christian got disbarred—he was taking kickbacks for funneling kids to Bennion's school.

Bennion, along with John, Rita and the others at the school were jailed.

The school was shut down, and the burial site and its contents seized by the Federal government.

But the rangers never could find the hunters setting traps below Roca Azul--there are too many of them out there—quiet as the dead.

When it comes to assholes—especially greedy ones—they're everywhere.

There are more acts of indifference, selfishness and cruelty than there are stars or seeds—galaxies or bones.

And more mysteries.

The behavior of fire, for example.

And wolves.

Dogs.

Stepdaughters.

And ghosts.

We haven't seen Gary, the yellow dog or the dead Indian again.

But I found out what a kill hole is—an opening made in pottery through which the dead pass into the afterlife.

It makes sense.

We each travel from life to death in our own way. So an opening in a clay pot or in the stone floor of an Indian ruin doesn't seem strange.

Our deaths are our own.

I had bullets.

Rose had cruelty and neglect.

The wolf had its trap.

Gary had a chokehold.

I hope wherever Gary went that he is not alone.

Rose has not left me again.

She remains unwaveringly brave and good.

Stoic.

Tranquil.

I wish you could see the buoyant grace with which she floats on her back right next to me—her eyes dreamy and affectionate—her paws relaxed as I give her a belly rub.

But I oscillate restlessly—moving from nowhere to nowhere again.

Should we go?

Or should we stay?

Returning to the world of the living is a shitty idea, isn't it?

Aren't two dismal lifetimes—mine and Rose's—and two return trips fucking enough?

But it's been a long time since Rose has seen a blade of grass.

A tree.

A bird in the air.

Clouds.

And she likes to look.

To pretend to sniff and to roll around.

She enjoys observing living animals.

Also there's someone I'd like to see.

"Rose," I say—my voice sounding thin and strange—"Come on."

Chapter 108

"Death ...doesn't seem too huge and terrible to let into your mind."

Rosie Thomas

It's early—an hour or so before the Desert Wildlife Rehabilitation Center opens to the public. Rose darts through one chain link enclosure to another—observing a bobcat, the raccoon, and a tortoise sunning itself.

The sight of the tortoise stops her. She drifts back in fear of the alien creature.

I coax her forward.

Rose follows me to a wide enclosed area dotted with craggy rocks and a few dry shrubs. In the corner is a low wooden structure with an opening. Three sleeping canine forms are visible on the flat roof.

When Rose discerns their shapes, she stops midair.

Her nostrils flare and she tries and fails to read and taste their scent.

Rose knows these animals. These are the orphaned wolf pups Cali rescued from Roca Azul.

Rose melts through the barrier as one of the smaller animals opens its eyes, stretches, yawns, and then jumps down and rolls lazily in the dirt—chin first.

Rose's wags her tail.

The wolf cub's fur is a thick yellowish dusty gray—almost the same color as the earth here. Its tail is long and thick with a black tip. Its eyes are amber outlined in black.

Now the other cubs wake.

They jump down and begin to wrestle, pinning each other and pretending to bite.

The cubs have grown to almost full size. Their dark coloring has faded.

A man stops at the edge of the enclosure and unlocks a small opening. He tosses large bones and hunks of raw meat inside and closes the opening in the fence.

The cubs stop playing and sniff the air, mouths open. Then they drag pieces of raw meat back to the rear area of the enclosure.

Rose watches them closely as they eat—her gaze earnest and resigned.

Chapter 109

"Life is beautiful. Death is astonishing."

Michael Biondi

We have one more stop, Rose and I—before we return to the afterlife.

At first I'm not sure I can find her—but there she is.

Cali.

There's my girl.

She's beautiful.

Her hair has grown to shoulder length—her natural auburn. The scratches on her face have healed and faded. Under the plain khaki pants and Greater Los Angeles Zoo beige t-shirt she wears, I can tell that she's gained some weight. She looks a little zaftig—strong and sure.

Rose and I drift close to her and I read her brown and white I.D. badge: "Cali Green, Junior Keeper. Greater Los Angeles Zoo."

Rose is overjoyed to see her. She sails like a butterfly in happy circles above Cali's head.

We hang around as Cali greets a group of visitors at the entrance, then leads the group through the Zoo grounds, stopping outside exhibits to talk about the animals and to answer questions.

Lowland Anoa.
Bongo.
Coati.
Tufted deer.

Just before the bat-eared fox enclosure, a woman in khaki shorts and a khaki shirt driving a golf cart slows the vehicle and waves at Cali. Cali waves back.

Ibex.
Lemur.
Meer cat.
Tapir.
Wallaby.
Wolf.

Cali stops at a wolf exhibit. It's out of the way in an area of low enclosures set behind the zebra barns.

"The Maned Wolf lives in the grasslands of Brazil and Argentina," Cali explains.

Rose floats to the enclosure's edge and then through the crisscrossed metal barrier.

"As you can see they have very long legs," Cali continues. "They are great climbers. These threatened animals are nocturnal and shy. They mate for life."

The long-legged wolf blinks at Cali from the back of the enclosure. Rose tries to sniff the animal's reddish coat. Weird, but Rose and this wolf are about the same size and same color.

A woman in the group who wears a straw hat raises her hand. Cali nods at her.

"What's killing them? What's killing the wolves?" she asks.

"We are," Cali says. "Farmers and hunters and trappers. Other wolf species are disappearing, too." Cali takes a paper from her back pocket and unfolds it. On it is a color photograph of a wolf that looks like the wolves that helped her to escape the fire.

"This is the Mexican Gray wolf. There used to be thousands, but there are only a few hundred left. They've been introduced to the wilderness areas of Arizona and New Mexico. The Mexican Gray Wolf is the most endangered land mammal in the United States. Some day—when I'm a vet— I'm going to help preserve them."

We follow Cali until she's completed the tour.

A few people thank her before walking toward the exits. Cali buys herself a soda at the snack bar, then trots up some stairs and into an office and writes her name on a sign-out sheet.

"I hear great things about you, Cali," a red haired woman in the office says and smiles. A sign on her desk says "Work-Study Program Coordinator." "How are you doing?"

"Good," Cali says and smiles, "Really good."

THE END

Also available from Fahrenheit Press

Dead Is Better by Jo Perry

CPSIA information can be obtained
at www.ICGtesting.com
Printed in the USA
LVOW11s1424121216
516919LV00002B/538/P